On Wings of Time

LINDA BOULANGER

Lochlainn Guardians: Book 1

On Wings of Time
©2017 by Linda Boulanger

Edited by Grace Augustine/Edits with a Touch of Grace
Cover Design/Interior Design by Tell~Tale Book Covers
First released as part of the Stoking the Flames: 13 Tales of Dragons, Destiny, & Desire Box Set

Published by TreasureLine Publishing

Also available in eBook publication

PRINTED IN THE UNITED STATES OF AMERICA

To Julia Mills...
Thank you for believing in me!

Chapter 1

Heart hammering, Amileigh McCollum tapped the heels of her boots to her horse's flanks. She hunkered low against his neck, not bothering to right the shoulder of her dress that had slipped off as they fled across the hillside.

"Run!" her companion had yelled. *"Don't stop until you get to the cave."*

Ami tried. She hadn't hesitated. She'd spurred her horse into action even before the dark shadows that covered their path momentarily blocked the sun. It wasn't until she'd heard the screeching cries that she'd looked back. The motion caused her to almost fall from her saddle, but she balanced herself just in time to slam right into the low-hanging branch of a tree.

Flying…
Floating…
Falling…

The world spun as limbs cracked and the smell of fresh turned earth churned around her. Cries and screeches overhead followed her down, drowning out the distressed groan parting her lips as she landed in a heap. Her dark-lashed lids fluttered then settled back over iced-lilac eyes that refused to stay open, not that she had the will to make them. She turned her head, the dirt beneath her grinding into the soft flesh of her ivory cheek and sticking in the massive blonde braid that trailed down to her waist. Her fingers scratched against the same earthen bedding. Was it not for the fury above her, Amileigh McCollum might have believed herself dead after being thrown from her horse. The thought that she'd been hurled into hell flashed through her mind, but she knew that wasn't the case. Something much more menacing was at play.

Where was her companion? Her heart jolted as his voice filled her head and the memory of the moments before rushed back—him telling her to run.

She'd tried to obey, riding like the devil himself was at her tail until the sounds behind her had lured her to glance back. Disbelief clouded her vision. What she'd seen could not have been real. Something, or some *things,* had been behind her. Their bellowing caws and guttural growls pulled her focus, making her forget to watch where she was going. She ran a hand over her chest and winced. She'd have a bruise for sure, but at least it hadn't been her head that had cracked against the branch and landed her in a heap on the ground.

No. Not on the ground, below it. She'd flown through the air coming down with a dull thud before the sound of breaking twigs and branches had accompanied another fall. This time she'd tumbled into a dark, earthen pit, her hand grazing its smooth side until she found herself sprawled on its rough bottom.

Ami tried to get up, fear rippled through her, queasiness gnawed at her insides. She stumbled back, sinking to her knees, her hands cushioning her head just before it hit the ground as she fell again and darkness engulfed her, pulling her from consciousness, away from the screaming battle above.

Kiernan.
Thoughts of her dear friend filled her head, jarring

Amileigh awake. She scurried to a sitting position and pushed a strand of hair away from her face. She listened to the silence above. Had Kiernan called her? Is that what had awakened her? She wished she could be assured he too had gotten away from the winged beasts bearing down on them.

Shivering, she ran a finger over her dry lips and shook her head. Her disheveled braid whispered against the silken over-material that covered her linen dress. He wasn't dead. If he was, she was certain she would feel it. And she couldn't. The problem was, she felt nothing. Nothing at all. She had the sense that she was floating nowhere and everywhere at the same time, her body suspended in an unsettling state of limbo.

Swiping at a tear that managed to roll down her dirtied cheek, Amileigh let her head loll back against the earthen wall of her cell. In the dim light, she looked around. This didn't look like one of the passageways to the underground caves beneath the hills around her home. It was too fresh and she could see no other way out than the opening above her head. If it was a trap, someone had surely put it in an idiotic place. What had they intended to trap, anyway? She looked up, guessing it hadn't been there long, otherwise the vegetation from above would have begun to make its way down the smooth surface of the walls.

With a sigh, she closed her eyes, letting exhaustion pull her into fitful sleep.

Clawing her way from the nightmare she'd been having about great winged creatures chasing her, Amileigh shivered at the thought of the decrepit beasts with their marred flesh that smelled of evil. Jagged razor-sharp teeth chipped and blackened in places from lack of care, and claws coated with filth and debris left over from their last battle... they had been so hideous she could barely look at them.

Not so with the dragon who flew before them. His unusual beauty drew her, commanding her eyes to stay on him. Covered with sparkling, glass-like scales—blue, purple, green—his beauty sparked a sense of nirvana deep inside her. Even at his enormous size, he still managed a graceful glide across the skies. Looking at him hadn't filled her with the dread and fear she'd felt from the others either. More, she'd felt nurtured, guarded. She sensed him standing between her and the others, knowing that as long as he was there, they couldn't harm her.

Not that they wouldn't try. For some reason, they'd wanted her badly. In the dream, the beautiful dragon had fought to keep them away while coaxing her, urging her to keep going. *Run*, he'd yelled at her. Only she had no idea where she was supposed to go or how long she was supposed to continue.

But she had run. As long as she could, as fast as her feet would carry her, until her arms began to feel heavy and her legs numb. As her strength began to wane, her heart pounded in fear that his would too. If she stopped or he failed...

Amileigh sat up, choking back a sob when she took in her surroundings, realizing her plight was real. Dear God, she thought. She had no idea what their task was or how they were to accomplish it, only that they *could not fail*. Something far greater than the two of them hung in the balance.

Sitting straighter, she pulled her knees to her chest and wrapped her arms around them wishing she'd taken the cloak her mother had suggested. The pit had grown chilly.

She looked up again and saw less light than before. It must be nightfall. Laying her cheek against her knee, she closed her eyes again wondering when they would come looking for her. She sighed. How many hours had it been? It seemed like years.

Loneliness pressed in around her until its weight lulled her into another restless sleep.

At some point Amileigh had laid down because when she woke she was curled into a fetal position, her arm a poor pillow beneath the right side of her face. Her attempted stretch was met with a grimace and surprise that her muscles were more stiff than sore. She frowned and pushed up to her knees before standing up the rest of the way and craning her neck skyward. At least it was day. Her family would surely be looking for her. They had to be worried sick.

Her frown deepened, concern contorting her pretty features as she stared at the upper walls of the pit. Goosebumps prickled her arms and she rubbed her hands up and down the sleeves of her gown. Where there had been no vegetation, lush vines now grew, drooping down the walls, stopping just beyond her reach. When she stepped forward, dried earth crunched beneath her feet, causing her to look down. She was surprised to see the leaves and other forest debris littering the pit's previously clean, packed floor, and the moistness in the dirt walls had given way to earth that broke into small fragments and fell at her touch.

Ami's heart beat wildly beneath the curved neckline of her gown. She spun in a slow circle taking in the newness of the old space. What had happened? There was no way it could have changed that quickly. Vines didn't grow where none had been, and ground deep within the earth didn't dry up and roughen overnight any more than... dragons roamed the skies.

Amileigh collapsed in a heap on the rubbish-laden floor, great sobs shook her entire body. What was happening? Why hadn't she heard the sounds of anyone looking for her? She wasn't *that* far from home and surely even if something had happened to Kiernan—perish the thought—her brothers would have thought to check the cave. She would have heard them riding by or calling out to her as they and the staff of Somerled fanned out to find her.

That's what they'd done when the smithy's daughter had disappeared two summers ago, and again when her brother's best broodmare had gone missing a few months back. They surely wouldn't leave *her* without even trying.

When her tears began to subside, Amileigh rolled to her back, not bothering to rein in the ragged breaths that came on the heels of her sobbing. She stared at the opening above her, growing dizzy from the feeling that the world was spinning much faster than it should be. Slowly, she closed her eyes, welcoming the darkness that once again invaded her mind.

Feather-light caresses tickled Amileigh's face, rousing her to just below the surface of consciousness. She tried to push away the offender. Her eyes fluttered several times before fully opening, the lilac orbs inside sparkling, even in the darkened depths of the pit. She sucked in hard when she looked around. While she'd slept, thick vines had crawled down the earthen walls, fanning out to form strange flooring.

Pushing up from the floor, Ami reached out only to draw her hand back. *Don't think. Act.* She had no choice.

Questioning the how and why of any of what had happened to her wasn't going to get her out of this hell.

She clenched her fists, then shook them out and grabbed one of the vines, giving it a yank to test its strength. The way they'd grown down, attaching to themselves and creating something of a nature-made netting, seemed anything but natural. They felt strange within her palms, smooth and almost cold, but without the give that one might expect from vegetation. They were nothing like the thick vines that grew up the West wall of Somerled Keep. She remembered times when she and her brothers had been instructed to help thin them, pulling them down so they wouldn't cover the few windows on that end of her family home.

With a deep breath, she pushed the memory away and raised her foot, only to have it tangle on the hem of her long skirt. She huffed and stepped back, her hands on her hips for a few seconds before she began to untie the ribbon at her waist and grabbed the hem of her underskirt, pulling it up to where it caught both the silk overlay and her linen dress. Tying it about her waist with the ribbon, she prayed no one would see her before she could get her legs covered.

The vines groaned and swayed, but didn't give way as she climbed. Half way up, she no longer cared if anyone saw her. Strong arms to pull her the rest of the way would have been an answered prayer, but no help came. With exhaustion threatening to send her back into the pit, she gave herself a mental slap and pushed her way through the overgrown shrubbery that hid her sunken cell, climbing free just as the earth beneath her began to shake. Amileigh stood on wobbly legs and stumbled farther away from the mouth of the pit, where she clung to the base of a tree until the ground finally stopped moving and she could push herself up.

With a sigh, she stood and looked around, trying to get her bearings. How long had it been since there'd been rumbling like that? They'd had a few tremors from time to time, but nothing that had lasted more than a few seconds. Kiernan had told her once of a legend that said the earth shook when the mighty dragons sleeping beneath rolled over, and that someday there would be a great shaking when they awakened and burst forth from their dirty graves. She shivered. She hadn't believed him then, telling him there were no such things as dragons. But did she believe him now? Had she truly seen winged creatures? Goosebumps pocked her arms as she fixed her skirts and brushed herself off. She needed to get home, to Somerled. Maybe then she would find her answers. Maybe then she'd find out this was all just a silly dream.

The dried grasses grabbed at the hem of Amileigh's long skirts, scratching at her legs beneath. She ignored them as best she could and trudged onward, fighting against a sense of heavy foreboding. She pressed her fingers to her temples, trying to alleviate the droning hum that had begun even before she'd clawed her way to freedom. The noise, she'd noticed, had intensified with every step she'd taken in the direction of Somerled.

Her heartbeat tripled when she topped the hill on the back side and caught sight of the old castle her family called home. Ami lifted her skirts with one hand, pushed back the long blonde curl that fell across her cheek, and quickened her pace. She should have secured her braid better, knowing that she and Kiernan would be galloping over the Lochlainn hillsides. She'd always loved their rides, loved the feel of the wind rushing around her letting her imagine she was almost flying. What she didn't love, at the moment, was Kiernan.

Amileigh slapped her free hand against her thigh thinking that's what she'd like to do to the man's face. Her nostrils flared and her lips now were a thin line. She still couldn't believe he'd left her confined in that hellish pit. She covered her heart. The foreboding remained, though not in connection with dear Kiernan Tavish.

He was still alive. She could feel him. But her family, her home... something had happened between the time she'd tumbled down into the pit and found her face against the coolness of the dank, earthy confines and now. The whirling of unanswered questions made her dizzy. She pushed away her concerns as she stopped on the perimeter of Somerled's lawn. Home, and the security that went with her life, stood before her.

Ignoring the uneasiness roiling inside her, Amileigh ran across the tamed section of the yard, the silence surrounding the castle sounding its loud, cautioning sentry salute. She ignored the nonexistent barking of the dogs that didn't greet her upon her return, as well as the lack of workers milling about. No one chopped wood or beat rugs. There were no servants' children playing on the back lawn like they usually did that time of day, no chickens tending to their busy work of scratching and clucking in the henhouse not far from the door that led to the kitchens... in fact, it wasn't until she took in the front of the house that she realized there had been no henhouse at all, just a pile of overgrown rubble.

Ami stepped around the corner. Her heart lodged in her throat, and she had to force herself to move forward. Tears welled in her eyes as she choked down the bile rising in her throat. She stepped onto the felled stones that should have comprised the entryway of her family's home. Beneath her feet, debris and grass replaced the imported Turkish flooring that had been brought in by boat and wagon. Her mother would have been devastated to see the smashed remnants of what little remained of her cuerda seca tiles, especially the large oval displaying the family crest in the center of the floor. No more of the floral patterns either— the stark contrast of soothing yellow and blue flowers edged in black, interspersed with the light gold hued tiles... rubble. Gone were the wooden furnishings and family heirlooms that should have welcomed her.

Disbelief clouded her vision as she turned slowly, moving closer to where the bottom of a grand staircase began. Hands and lips shaking, she reached toward one of the few remaining walls. The stones, cold beneath her fingers, felt much as they had the last time she'd touched them. She closed her eyes, envisioning herself racing back up the stairs to get her riding gloves, her fingertips trailing along the stones. Only there were no stairs to grant her passage upward now. The lovely banister her father had commissioned to fulfill her mother's dream... gone. And her family? They surely weren't there, but were they gone as well? She closed her eyes, resting her forehead against the stones, trying to sense some form of life. All she felt was the vibration from the continued droning hum in her head. And... voices?

Amileigh sucked in, the sharp breath nearly making her cough. Her eyes went wide when she heard the sound again and realized the owners of the voices were coming closer. Covering her mouth just in time to muffle the cough, she hurried to the hidden cutout right inside the hallway that led to what had been her father's study and the library beyond.

The yellow drawing room and doors that opened to a

rose garden had been down there as well. It was all gone, except for the section of the wall that held the tiny alcove. Its purpose had been to secret away servants from the view of guests passing down the hall. Amileigh had used it to hide from a justly irate parent or to spy on unsuspecting visitors when she was a small child. Now it would provide cover so she could hear and possibly see without the owners of the voices knowing she was there.

"Put your shirt on, you ass. Nobody wants to look at all that skin. Even if it is covered by some pretty amazing ink."

Amileigh frowned. *Ink*? Why would it be on his skin?

The other voice made some scoffing noises before commenting. "Don't give me that, Mairi. You know you love it. You're probably wettin' your jeans just thinking about running your tongue over every last inch of..."

"Shut up, you dick. We both know there's only one Tavish brother I want to run my tongue over. And he sure as hell ain't you."

Tavish! Amileigh didn't care who they were or what they were saying. She could sort all that out later. But, if this guy was a Tavish, he would surely know where Kiernan was.

The man's laughter and response trailed off when she stepped from the narrow slit in the wall, his mouth froze on his unspoken word.

Amileigh frowned. She didn't recognize him, and his odd attire was concerning. She looked at the female wearing tight fitting pants and a shirt that looked much like it should have been an undergarment. But when her gaze turned back to the man, she found herself studying him from top to bottom, starting with the thick, dark hair that looked like he'd rolled out of bed and ran his fingers through it and nothing more. It was very much like Kiernan's, though not quite as kempt. His eyes were the same odd piercing blue. There was no way the two men could not be related.

When her eyes darted to the fullness of his still parted lips, she forgot what she needed to know. His biceps rippling beneath his pale, peachy-pink long-sleeved shirt didn't help either. It hung open revealing hard planes and toned muscles... and some sort of a design that appeared etched into his skin. *Ink*?

Her mouth watered and her tongue darted out to share that moisture with her dry lips. How many women had traced that design with their tongues? The thought had Amileigh's face turning crimson red and she grimaced at the smirk she was sure she saw when she glanced briefly into his eyes before looking downward and wishing she hadn't.

Below the waist, he was clothed in a rather form-fitting peculiar blue dyed material. What had he said to the woman? Something about her wetting her jeans. Since they were both wearing the same material, they must be the jeans he referred to. Wearing them wet sounded quite uncomfortable... every bit as uncomfortable as she was growing, though that discomfort was overshadowed by the humming in her head that was beginning to come in great waves very nearly blotting out all the sounds of the outdoors.

"Who are you?" Amileigh's words were a breathy whoosh. "And what are you doing in my house?"

"What the hell?" The woman's voice swirled about Ami's swaying form. "I don't know who you are or where you came from, Cinderella, but we're not the ones trespassing. These ruins and the beautiful castle that stood here before them have been in my family since... practically forever. At least since the thirteen to fourteen hundreds. So, I'm guessing it's us who should ask who the hell are you?"

Amileigh slowly shook her head, trying hard to keep her eyes focused on the girl the man had called Mairi. "Your family? That can't be. This is… Somerled, owned by my family, the McCollum's. The lands were bestowed upon my great, great grandfather by the king himself. I am… I am Amileigh McCollum. Gairlich McCollum's only daughter." She managed a slow-eyed change of view from the woman to the man. "Please." The word was rushed, the rest barely audible. "Kiernan Tavish. Do… do you… know him?" One hand to her temple, Amileigh used the other against the wall to steady herself as the sound inside her mind grew continually louder.

"Kiernan?" The man looked bewildered. "Of course, I know him. He's my great grandfather."

Amileigh stared at him, the world around them began to swim. "Merciful heavens. That can't be. He's but a few years older than..." She looked up as a dark shadow blotted out the sunlight above. "…me," she finished before falling back against the stone wall and sliding to the ground, her head missing a pile of rubble only by the quick movements of Lukas Tavish who cushioned the blow with a dive and outstretched hands.

Chapter 2

Familiar sounds and smells greeted Amileigh as she clamored from yet another restless sleep. She looked around her, startled to find herself in her own bed, everything as it should be. Everything except her body. She turned her head toward the window, and winced at the pain that grabbed her shoulders and ran clear to the tips of her toes. Goodness, she hadn't felt this bad since she was a child and had fallen into a hole that led down into the caves beneath Somerled. It was the first time she'd learned they were there. Fortunately, the wall had sloped in instead of opening up to drop her all the way to the cavern floor and her brothers and Kiernan had been there to rescue her.

Kiernan!

She sat up too quickly, uncertain whether to grab her spinning head or collapse against her body's protest. She did neither, instead whipping back the white coverlet and swinging her legs over the side of the tall bed. Sliding off the mattress and landing on shaky legs, Amileigh ignored the throbbing between her temples. The dull hum was another matter. She felt almost as if it was pulling her or directing her steps. But to where?

It took her a while, but she made her way to the door where she rested her head against the dark plank. Her dry tongue tried to satisfy even drier lips to no avail and she looked back to the cup that sat on the table beside her bed. As weak as she felt she wasn't sure she'd be able to make it back to the door if she went for the cup, but without something to quench the fire in her throat she'd be unable to call for anyone once she gained access to the hallway.

Why had she not thought of the water before she left her bed? Why did she feel so weak? Was she ill? That was the only explanation why her body ached and strange visions clouded her mind. Dragons! No one believed in them, except maybe small children and the daft... and her? Ami couldn't shake how real it had seemed when she'd dreamed about turning to see the dragons in the sky behind her. The sound of their wings, their large bodies soaring through the currents of air... she'd heard it above the pounding of her horse's hooves. And over that incessant hum. Although it wasn't as loud as it was when she'd collapsed—if that had actually happened—the hum refused to go away.

Ami reached up to touch her forehead, willing her mind to quiet, but when her toe caught on the hem of her gown, she went down. She had moved close enough to the bed to catch the skirting around her nightstand. As she fell, she pulled the full glass of water, the pitcher, and all her baubles off as she went. She wasn't sure if she'd screamed, but the commotion brought the sound of running feet and a flurry of arms attempting to untangle her from the mess. She was grateful for the familiarity when one set of arms in particular won out and her brother lifted her, cradling her to him for a split second before plopping her unceremoniously onto the bed. Ami fought to roll to the other side.

"Ami! What are you doing? Be still before you hurt yourself more. You're acting like a numbskull." Her twin's voice was demanding, though even Auley's deep scowl didn't cover his concern.

Amileigh ignored it and glared back at him from the opposite side of the bed. "Me a numbskull? When you'd have me ruin the coverlet with this wet gown? Mother would have both of our heads."

Her brother rolled his eyes that were a darker purple than her own with a strong hint of blue. Straightening, he backed away from the opposite side of the bed, still staring at her. One would not have expected someone with such fair hair and complexion to have the ability to look so stern, but the McCollum men had mastered it. Had it been anyone but Ami that he fixed with his glare, the person might well have been quaking. Instead, she scoffed back, measuring whether it was worth moving from the bedside so she could turn her back in a show of open defiance.

Auley offered a huffed chuckle, turning to the two other women in the room and blowing out a loud breath before speaking. "It appears her run in with the stranger has caused no change in her usual dour behavior."

Ami's sharp intake of air had him wheeling back to stare at her again.

"Stranger?" she whispered, her eyes going wide. "You mean… 'twas not a dream?"

One of the other women—her lady's maid, shook her head. "No, milady. We feared greatly for you, what with no one ever having seen the likes of him before, and him dressed and behaving so oddly. We thought…"

"Where is he now, the stranger?" Amileigh cut her off.

"Deep in the belly of the castle, where he belongs. He's obviously a madman." Her brother's features hardened even more, making him look every bit as stern as her father.

Feeling her knees go weak, Amileigh grabbed for the wooden post at the foot of her bed. She leaned against it, the coolness welcomed against her heated face. She clenched her teeth, fighting to breathe. She sensed more than felt Auley move to her side and wasn't surprised that not only was he there, but he'd dismissed the other women from the room. They left with a grumble and inside, Amileigh smiled. Her mother had always said her twins could read one another, most likely from having shared a womb together.

Without him speaking, Ami knew her brother's question. "Brother, please. Go and fetch Kiernan. What I have to say needs to be said to him and no other."

Auley scoffed. "Why is everyone asking for Kiernan? First the stranger, then father. Now you. What does he have to do with all of this?"

Ami shook her head, her loose blonde curls whispering against her night dress. "Something's happening, Aul, and I don't know what. But..." She contemplated sharing everything with him—the pit, the dragons, Somerled in ruins, the ceaseless hum... She pressed against her head with her palms on either side and sat back against her bed. "Please, Aul. Just... get him."

The weight of the mattress dipped when he sat down beside her and Amileigh leaned against her brother. He slipped an arm around her, patting her shoulder much as he had to comfort her when they were children. "He's already on his way, Ami. Should be but a few more moments. I'll have him sent to you as soon as he's finished speaking to father."

"No!" She pulled away and stood to face him, her eyes wide. "I must speak to him first. You have to find him and make sure he comes to speak to me before any other."

Auley stood slowly, his palms facing forward in front of him, much as one might approach a crazed or troubled person. "It's fine," he practically cooed. "I'll find him. You can trust me."

Having heard him use that same tone on a skittish horse or a spooked dog, Ami bristled. Brows drawn tight, nose crinkled, and mouth turned downward, she glared at him. "Stop it, Auley. Just do as I ask." She stomped her bare foot and crossed her arms, turning toward the window just in time to see the dark shadow sweep past it. Cold fingers raced up her spine and she spun back to try to catch Auley's reaction. He was still looking at her as if he had no idea where his sister had gone. True, her behavior had been rather erratic in the time since she'd awakened. Whose wouldn't be when confronted with the very real possibility of racing through time, seeing the future, and being chased by dragons? But if that shadow was any indication, that was exactly what had happened and if Kiernan was alone... "How many men rode out to escort Kiernan?" Ami asked her brother.

"What?" Auley shook his head. "I don't know. One maybe... the messenger. Or perhaps two in case they had to split off. I really don't have any idea. Why?"

"Because," Ami spoke in a quiet voice, turning back toward her window. "I fear his life may be in danger."

"Yet he is here." Kiernan's voice filled her room and both occupants turned to see him walking through the door, his smile wide, teeth white against his sun-kissed complexion.

"Kiernan!" Ami practically squealed. Finding strength to overcome her weakness, she ran around the bed and wrapped her arms around his neck, sighing when she felt his arms encircle her. In her relief over his safety, she hadn't stopped to think of how unseemly it was for a lady dressed only in her night dress to be in such close proximity to a man not her husband. At least she hadn't until a cleared throat pulled her attention to the doorway. She looked up into the eyes of her father, and stepped away from Kiernan almost as quickly as he released her. They both froze under the icy glare of the Lord of Somerled.

A man of no small stature, Gairlich McCollum's presence overwhelmed the open door. He made a slow perusal of the room's occupants, disapproval pulling at his brows and causing the muscle of his cheek to twitch.

"Abigail!" he bellowed, his gaze raking down Ami's body dressed in the thin material of her sleeping gown made even thinner by the water she'd spilled on herself.

Ami wrapped her arms across her body, feeling suddenly exposed, and watched as her young lady's maid materialized behind her father.

"Ye... yes, milord?"

Gairlich stepped back, grunting when the girl dropped into a deep curtsy fit for the King himself. No matter how many times he'd told his staff a simple bob would do, they continued with full salute. Ami figured it was in part to his ranking with the King, though most assuredly his thunderous demeanor made up the rest. Had the moment been less serious, Ami would have laughed at Abigail's visible wince when the girl rose on her father's grumbled command.

"Fetch my daughter a wrap at once. Something that will aptly cover her."

Her father's words had everyone looking in Ami's direction and her cheeks flaming. She envisioned herself looking much like one of the statues in the King's forbidden garden that she and her brothers had sneaked into when she was barely fifteen. The garden was rightfully named Xardín do Amor—the Garden of Love, designed to create *the mood*. As she aged, Ami realized that *mood* was seduction. The fragrant flowers, secluded shrubbery alcoves, pergolas with their soft as a bed grass flooring, and the statues... half-naked women, couples engaged in various states of entanglement. Even at her young age, Ami had felt the budding need building inside her as she'd walked through the space.

At first, she'd thought the flittering in her middle was caused by the fear of getting caught in a place she wasn't supposed to be. But that fear was quickly replaced by a heated headiness, a feeling of being disconnected or floating. She'd begun wandering openly then, studying the statues, each statue stealing her breath even more than the one before. One statue in particular, had never left her mind. The man, his hard planes chiseled into the white stone, stared adoringly down at the woman in his arms. The woman also looked down, watching his fingers forever caressing the side of her breast, exposed by her partially removed gown.

Ami had thought of that statue over the years, the likeness of the man replaced by whomever she fancied at the time, the woman always her. Even now the image caused her breasts to peak and tendrils of desire to lap at her middle. She looked down, pressing her arm more firmly over her chest and held her legs tighter together. It didn't help that the last man she'd replaced the cold stone with was now standing beside her, his body heat radiating into her arm so close to his. Ami welcomed the thick wrap her maid draped over her shoulders. She pushed her arms through the side openings and made a show of cinching the ends of the ribbons that Abigail pushed through to her on either side to give her downturned face more time to cool off.

"Thank you, Abigail. You may leave us now." The maid scurried toward her father even before his words were done. Dropping a quick curtsy, she vanished. Ami frowned. The girl obviously feared for her position. She should never have left Amileigh alone in her chambers with a man. Never mind that her brother was there and it was Kiernan. Men were not allowed in a Lady's bedroom. Ami wished she could reassure the girl, but more pressing matters prevailed. There was that stranger in the dungeon that held the key to whatever was going on.

"Father! I must speak to Kiernan." Wide lilac eyes implored the man in the doorway.

His brows still drawn, Gairlich stepped in and began to close the door.

"No, Father." Her words stopped his motion. "In private. Alone."

Her father paused for only a moment before he slammed the door the rest of the way into its frame and turned to face his daughter. "What in God's good name is going on here?" His icy glare blasted her and then Kiernan, flicking briefly to Auley who still stood on the far side of the bed, before landing back on his daughter. "First you are attacked by some madman going on about being from a different time, then your mother reports you crying out in your sleep about dragons and being trapped. And now..." His lips thinned and nostrils flared as he again looked at them one by one. He didn't have to finish for them to understand.

Amileigh swallowed the lump in her throat and commanded her heavy legs to take her across the room. She stopped directly in front of her father. "Please, Father," she said softly, placing her palm against his chest. "You know I wouldn't ask if it wasn't truly important. I know the implications and how all of this must look."

She stared up at him, watching him war against reason and propriety, hopeful his love and concern for her would win out. After what seemed like an eternity, he nodded.

"You have three minutes. And I shall be standing right outside the door." He glared at Kiernan. "You are to stand apart from my daughter, and if you ever disobey my orders again, you may consider yourself unwelcome in my house. Is that clear?"

Kiernan took a step back though quickly masked his shock. He nodded. Only his clenched fists showed he remained wounded by the words from the man Ami knew he held in as much esteem as if he'd been his own father.

Amileigh held her tongue until just before the door closed after her brother skirted past and rushed out. "Father." She waited until her father widened the opening of the doorway and stared back. Words weren't needed for her to know he expected her to continue. "Tis not Kiernan's fault. I demanded his audience..."

"Ami, no..."

Kiernan's protest was overridden by her father's. "Men should not play host to a woman's folly." He shook his head. "Even if your claim was true, Lord Tavish should have known better than to disregard *my* orders."

Amileigh snorted. "Would that I might live to see a time when such chauvinistic ways do not prevail."

The lord of Somerled narrowed his eyes at his only daughter. "Until that time, Amileigh, you will do well to watch your tongue." Even the air stilled as the two stared at one another. "If you wish to have the privilege of speaking to Kiernan as you desired, I suggest you stop with these foolish notions of yours." He ignored her eye roll and looked at Kiernan. "Three minutes."

No sooner had the door closed than both Kiernan's and Amileigh's stares were drawn to the window, her head snapping in that direction a fraction of a second slower than his... enough for her to confirm her thoughts.

"You saw it too."

Kiernan stiffened as she walked the few steps to stand directly before him. When she put her hands on his biceps, he shook his head and tried to step back, but Ami held firm.

"Your father's words, Ami," he whispered, glancing toward the door.

"Kiernan, please. Tell me what's going on." Her tone matched his. "You saw the shadow, did you not?" She shook his sleeves when he looked away instead of answering and he finally nodded. "How can this be?"

"I'll explain everything later, but first I need to know about the man. Tell me what you remember."

Ami nodded, her breath catching as she opened her mouth to speak. "It was after I got back to Somerled. I hid in the alcove by my father's study when I heard the voices. He and the woman came around the corner. They were talking and I tried to listen but the humming in my head was becoming unbearable. She called him Tavish and I thought he must know you. Only he said Kiernan Tavish was his great grandfather. Then everything was spinning again like it was when I was in the pit..."

Kiernan interrupted. "The pit?"

Amileigh nodded. "The one I fell into when we were riding. The earth shook and the sky began to rumble behind us. You told me to ride to the cave and not look back. But I did. I'm sorry, Kiernan, but the sounds..." Her eyes filled with tears. "The great beasts..." She covered her face with her hands, a small sob escaping her.

Kiernan pulled her into an embrace and she continued, her forehead on his chest. "They chased us... chased me. You were no longer there." She looked up at him through glistening eyes, then reached up to touch his cheek with tear-moistened fingers. She traced his brow line, circling his eye. "The beautiful one—the creature in the lead... his eyes..."

"I'll explain later." Kiernan grabbed her wrists, bringing her hands to his chest. "This ride... when did it happen?"

Her face crinkling in confusion, Ami shrugged. "Do you not remember, Kiernan? It was Sunday afternoon. We'd talked at the King's supper about how much I wanted to ride out and explore the cave again and you said I should not go alone, that you'd take me at the week's end. Only you were detained so we had to postpone until the next week." His frown prompted her to continue. "Do you not remember the picnic Mother had packed for us? How we were racing across the hills, laughing before the rumbling began?"

Kiernan took a deep, exaggerated breath but didn't answer her. "What did you see when you returned to Somerled?"

Ami's look grew far away. "I must have hit my head because I believed everything to lay in rubble. That's why I hid in the alcove until he said your name, especially since they were dressed so oddly and spoke of peculiar things." She switched her gaze back to him."

"Did the humming in your head get louder when he got closer?" Ami nodded and Kiernan mirrored it. "And when you touched..."

"No. We didn't touch. At least I don't think..." She frowned. She vaguely remembered him moving toward her as her world faded around her. *Her world.* She hadn't been in her world, had she? She'd been in his. How was that even possible? She looked to Kiernan.

"What was the date, Ami?"

She told him, her eyes swimming again at his frown. "Kiernan?" She'd never seen him so somber. Fear prickled her skin, especially when her window darkened again.

"My trip, Ami… I just returned yesterday and today is Tuesday. All you have spoken has not yet taken place."

A knock on her door froze them both. Kiernan shook his head when she started to speak.

"Get dressed," he told her, giving her hands a light squeeze before releasing her. "Stay in your room, do you understand?" When she nodded, he continued. "I'll send for you, but leave only with myself. Or Auley," he added. She nodded again and he crossed the room, pausing with his hand on the door handle. He glanced back at her, a sad smile lifting the corners of his mouth. "Abra was right. With your parentage, you were bound to be the chosen Prihom. I just couldn't quite accept it, especially since I could sense no others of my kind. But she was right."

"Who is Abra?" Ami asked his retreating back. His answer was the closing door. "And what's a… Prihom?" she whispered as she slowly turned away.

Chapter 3

Abigail appeared seconds later with another pitcher of water and began pulling Amileigh's garments from the larger wardrobe in the corner. After a few more seconds, Ami shook herself from the stunned stupor, unwrapped her arms from the bedpost and pushed herself up from the mattress where she'd slumped after Kiernan had left. She tried to make sense of all he'd said and all that had happened, but it was too much. Ignoring it, she walked over to the wardrobe Abigail had just closed. With her hands on the wardrobe knobs, she opened the doors and stared blankly at its contents.

"Do you not wish to wear what I have chosen, milady?" Abigail's voice sounded softly over her shoulder. Ami almost never contradicted whatever garments her maid chose for her to wear. It usually didn't matter to her.

She shook her head. "I'm sure it's fine. I just want to see..." She pulled away from the wardrobe, and smothered the gasp that rose in her throat. Hanging in the wardrobe's center was the gown she'd worn on her ride with Kiernan. It was as fresh and clean as it had been when they'd brought it home from the dressmaker's cottage.

"This one?" She asked Abigail, running her fingers down its side, "have I worn it yet?" She swallowed the lump in her throat.

"No, Mistress. Would you like me to switch..."

Ami cut her off with a forceful no and slammed the wardrobe doors closed. She ignored Abigail's wide eyes. She knew her behavior was odd, but to be honest, she didn't care. For once, she really didn't. Something was happening and she felt certain her life was about to be torn apart.

"Be quick, Abigail," she told the servant as she began to remove her robe and wet gown. "Kiernan said to be ready. I need to hurry." She didn't know where Kiernan had gone, other than to speak to her father, but she had the feeling he wouldn't be long. Nothing would hold her back when Auley came to fetch her, whether she had a dress on or not.

Kiernan had been surprised to see Auley outside Amileigh's door instead of her father. He'd breathed out a sigh of relief. He loved Gairlich McCollum almost as a son would his own father, but the man could be downright frightening at times. Kiernan suppressed a chuckle. No one knew how much older he was than the Lord of Somerled... other than that lord, Abra, and himself. Gairlich still treated him the age he looked, and Abra... She'd lived a half year more than he had

His chest tightened when he thought of his beloved. He'd been away from her far too long. If he was correct, he'd be returning to her side within a fortnight, or sooner. He smiled, his head tilted down so that no one saw. They might mistake what brought about his smile. Not that he didn't care deeply for Amileigh. He did. He'd even say he loved her... just not in the way he loved Abra. Amileigh was not his, Abra was. Now, what he needed to find out was whether his hunch was right and Amileigh was the Prihom—the key that would unlock the dragon within the man held in the bowels of Somerled. His only hope was that Gairlich would listen.

Rapping his knuckles on the door, Kiernan waited until the voice on the other side bid him to enter. He pushed open the door to see Gairlich McCollum standing at the window on the far side of the room, his hands locked behind his back as he stared out at the land that had belonged to his family for centuries. Kiernan didn't speak, only waited and watched.

"She's my only daughter. My youngest child. I don't want to lose her."

Kiernan began to make a joke about her being the youngest by mere minutes, but the pained expression on Gairlich's face when the man turned toward him stopped the foolish jest. He and Abra had parented many children, most who left the world as mere mortals because the dragons in their blood hadn't been released or no Blend was found that needed their feminine magic to transform. They'd led happy, fulfilled lives. Just not the lives they were destined to lead.

He looked at Gairlich. Yes, he knew the anguish more than he'd have liked. But he also knew what awaited Amileigh if she was a Prihom who had not only met a dragon, but *the* dragon destined for her. That thought thrilled him. No greater love would exist for her, no greater fulfilment.

And for Kiernan? Finally, the fight would no longer be his alone.

Gairlich shuffled to the large desk not far from the window and slumped into the seat. "Can we be sure he's not one of *them*?"

The *them* Gairlich referred to were the Dubhagan—the dark dragons who wanted to rule the world, making men their slaves instead of their equals. No, they both knew there were no guarantees. Many of the Nebrani Prihoms had been taken in days of old, their powers used to unlock the dragons of the Dubhagan, the women basically used as breeding stock. Their offspring may have been of diluted and mixed blood, but pairing them with other captured or bred Prihoms still produced dragons.

Eventually, the Dubhagan had begun to die off as well. Their inferior genetics had not guaranteed longevity and their numbers had dwindled, just as Kiernan's band had, due to deaths in battle, life, and simply growing too old to continue. He thought of King Nicolai and felt the old dragon stir within him. Nicolai Ruthven was one of the few Dragons of Kedan whose spirit had infused into a Guardian instead of passing his essence on through the blood. He'd chosen Kiernan, even though he was already an unlocked dragon, the essence of a long-ago dragon having passed to him through his bloodline and unlocked by his Prihom, Abra. It seemed complicated, but it wasn't. Kiernan continued to be his own dragon and that particular beast took over when he shifted. King Nicolai only operated in his mind, his wisdom guiding Kiernan through the centuries so that they might both live to see the Kedan Dragons victorious.

But to do that, he needed to find out what was going on. Why had Amileigh experienced a time shift? Six days wasn't a lot, but the fact that she saw Somerled in ruins in that time was greatly disturbing. He'd long believed the Keep was enchanted. At least there was some great energy that he felt every time he came near.

"I need to speak to this man that claims he is my kinsman. Do I have your permission, Gairlich?"

Gairlich McCollum steepled his hands, tapping his pursed lips with the two extended fingers. After several seconds of looking off into an imagined distance, and without looking at Kiernan, he nodded. "Be sure, Kiernan. I'm not keen to this whole idea, and Lord help us all if her mother should decide we're wrong."

Again, Kiernan stifled a chuckle. Lady McCollum was no kitten where her children were concerned. Like Abra, she too was of pure Prihom bloodline—one of the few female Pures born in the last few centuries. The fact that she'd married Gairlich—another Pure, though male, should have alerted him that something was coming... or *someone*. That someone being Amileigh.

When two daughters had been born after so long... the mothers of Saundra and Gairlich... King Nicolai had told Kiernan to be on guard. He'd done just that, guarding the two women to a fault until they were both married to other Nebrani. He'd searched for their dragons to no avail. When Lady Saundra had been born, he'd again set to guarding her while working to find her dragon. It was then he'd begun to wonder if he was the last of the Dragons of Kedan, a completely devastating feeling settling in the pit of his stomach. If only he'd had a son at the time.

Abra had assured him all would work out and in its own time. He smiled. His Abra—forever the eternal optimist. She had told him to watch over Amileigh, even though it meant a continuation of their time apart. "You're a Kedan Dragon, Kiernan, a Guardian of Lochlainn, with a King living inside you. You have a responsibility that goes beyond the two of us." She'd snuggled into him, looking up through her dark lashes with blue eyes forever dancing with mischief. "Do you not remember the words you spoke at our binding, my love? When you swore not only to love me forever, but to do your part to preserve the future generations of Lochlainn... both dragon and Prihom?" She'd laughed, a rich, throaty sound that even now ran sparks of desire through him. "You've always known there was more to that than simply producing children with me. Though before you leave…" She'd pulled his mouth down to hers, her hands already working the fasteners of his tunic. "Perhaps we will have a son."

Kiernan had laughed. "Perhaps, though she'd be too old for him."

Abra had slapped him on the chest. "Nonsense! Older women are fascinating."

Considering that Abra was his senior… even if only by six months… and that she was nearly 300 years old now, he couldn't agree with her more. "I do believe you grow more fascinating by the day." He'd sucked in a breath and groaned when her hand slid into his britches, grabbing the evidence of his desire. "And bolder, too." With her other hand, she'd pushed the material over his hips before following it toward the floor. On her knees in front of him, she'd kissed the head he thought with most often when he was with her. Without pretense, he'd whipped the tunic and blouse off so that he could watch her, unobstructed, after the first time her tongue had flicked out to taste his glistening tip.

Kiernan looked up to see Gairlich staring at him and realized he'd been reminiscing much too long. He could only hope he hadn't made a spectacle of himself by moaning at the thought of Abra's warm mouth wrapped around him just seconds before he'd pulled her up and plunged fully into her moist depths. With a shake of his head, he thanked God that women wore no undergarments in that day, having given up the unnecessary subligaculum of the Roman era.

"Perhaps you would like me to accompany you?" Gairlich pushed a hand through his thick, lightly graying bronze curls and looked almost relieved when Kiernan shook his head.

"I think it will go better if I'm alone." When Gairlich nodded, he turned toward the door. "I'll return as soon as I'm done."

"Kiernan."

Kiernan stopped and looked back at Gairlich. He wished he could get rid of the anguish in the man's eyes. When Somerled's Lord didn't speak again, Kiernan did. "Have you seen him, my Lord?"

Gairlich nodded and glanced away before looking directly in Kiernan's face. "He has your eyes."

Chapter 4

Kiernan heard the man railing the guard, even before he descended the last of the stone steps. Some of the words were unfamiliar, though their intent was unmistakable. He stifled a chuckle before rounding the corner and rendering both guard and caged man silent. It wasn't so much that he found humor in the situation as it was that he somehow expected it, especially if this man was of Tavish descent.

"You'll not earn yourself any favor berating those who hold the key to your freedom, you know." The two men locked eyes as Kiernan moved further into the area outside the cell.

The man snorted. "You sound like my grandfather." He shifted from one foot to the other, his head cocked as he studied Kiernan. "Who are you anyway? I feel like we've met before."

Kiernan raised a brow as he stared back. There was no doubt they were related, though exactly how, he was uncertain. There was a definite resemblance, and although they weren't replicas of each other, the man could certainly have passed for one of his brothers... if he had an older brother. A distant cousin, perhaps? Though if that was the case... disappointment attempted to creep in. It would mean the man had no dragon blood and his hope for himself, for Amileigh, and for their kind would be squashed.

Still not answering the question, Kiernan turned and asked the guard to leave them, which the man did after no more than a moment's hesitation. Had it been anyone else, Kiernan was sure the man would not have relented. Thankfully, those who served under Lord McCollum knew

Kiernan well enough to know he would never act without the man's approval. He watched the guard, listened for his footsteps to quiet and the massive door at the top of the steps carved into the dirt beneath the castle to open and close. Turning back, he kept his eyes averted, closing them and breathing deeply, his fists clenching and releasing.

"What are you doing? Did you not hear me ask who you are?"

Kiernan ignored the prisoner. *What should I do, my King?* He waited for the direction of the mighty beast within his head. *How will I know if this man is friend or foe? I'm lost here. So much is at stake. I don't know…*

Silence, young Kiernan. Be still. Feel. You will know. The words of the dragon king formed in his mind.

"Hey!"

"Shhh." After a few more seconds, Kiernan lifted his head and smiled, sure he probably appeared insane to the captured man. But he'd done as King Nicolai had directed and felt what he needed to feel. His own dragon stirred inside, elated by the nearness of another of his own kind.

"The better question," Kiernan began, walking closer to the cage, "is do you, my young friend, have any idea who you are?"

The man stood at the bars, his hands tightly wrapped around the cold metal, his eyes never wavering as Kiernan approached. Kiernan stopped just out of reach.

"What's your name?"

The wary captive raised a single dark brow. "Pretty sure I asked you first."

Kiernan threw back his head and laughed. He liked this man. His spunk and wit would serve him well in all he had to do. Reigning in his mirth, he gave one more half chuckle. "If I'm not mistaken," he told the man before turning toward the stairs, "I'd say I'm your great grandfather." He crossed the floor in a few steps and began taking the dirt-packed stairs two at a time.

"What the..." he heard the prisoner yell. "Hey! Where you going? You can't just leave me here!"

"I'll be back," he called down.

"My name's Luke. Lucas Tavish. Will that get me out any faster?" A moment of silence was followed by a string of muttered curses.

The man was slumped against the bars when Kiernan reentered the holding room. "Lucas?" Kiernan nodded, then whispered, "Loukas—the bringer of light... Your name is written in the books."

"What books?"

"Never mind that for now. Is there any way you can prove who you are?"

The man, Lucas, was already nodding, though he let loose another string of curses as he pressed his hand into his back pocket then the front. "Damnit to hell! Mairi said I should give her my wallet and phone when I ripped my pocket. My ID and everything was in there. I've got nothing... except..." He reached into his other front pocket and pulled out something that looked like a thin, silver coin. He held it up and looked squarely at Kiernan. "My great grandfather told me no matter what, to never be without this." He handed it to Kiernan. "He said someday it might very well save my life."

Kiernan studied the thin metal. None of it meant much to him. Judging by its weight, it couldn't be worth much either. Then he noticed something. Along the bottom edge on one side was a date. The numbers 2016 rose from the metal. He lifted his eyes to the man. "This number. What is it?"

"Each year, Grandpa Kiernan has had me replace the coin with a new one. That number," he motioned to the coin, "reflects the current year."

Kiernan nodded, staring back at the coin's face. "Two thousand and sixteen," he whispered before looking up. "It appears you have traveled back nearly six hundred years to meet your destiny."

Luke started to scoff, then looked around. He still didn't know what was going on, but arguing with the man who claimed to be his great grandfather, even though he was younger, not to mention that the span of six hundred years didn't add up... no, something was wrong with the whole thing, but arguing those points weren't going to help him. That much he knew.

Relief washed over him when the younger Kiernan handed his coin back.

"It doesn't help with the who, but perhaps the when. I have to go speak to the Lord of the Keep now, but I'll be back," Kiernan told him. It was obvious by the way Kiernan's eyes darted about he was trying to figure out everything as well. Luke stepped back and nodded. What else could he do?

"Don't forget me," he charged.

Kiernan chuckled and tapped his temple. "Memorable men are not soon forgotten."

Luke sucked in a startled breath. Those were the same words his great grandfather had used throughout his childhood.

With a nod, Kiernan turned and left him alone again. Luke looked at the coin in his hand, tossing it up a couple of times before slipping it back into his pocket.

The creaking of the heavy door at the top of the stairs was followed by hard footfalls pounding against the steps. Luke stopped his pacing and moved back to the bars. He wasn't surprised the person who entered the holding area a few seconds later wasn't Kiernan, though he was surprised when the burly man dressed in leather and fur didn't so much as lift his head to look in his direction as he crossed the space to another door on the far end of the room.

"He...hey!" he managed just before the man's massive hands closed on the thick ring handle and heavy plank used to keep in whatever was behind that door. He had to suppress a shiver when the man turned toward him, the battle-damaged face bringing up forgotten boyhood images of one of the Hagan brothers leering at him from above as he administered face numbing blows. This man had obviously seen far worse, but his dark eyes and scraggly features held an uncanny resemblance. Frowning, Luke continued. "Kiernan Tavish. Any sign of him up there? He's supposed to be coming to get me out of here."

His hand now fondling the end of the whip attached to one side of his belt, the man took two steps toward Luke's cell. "He tell ye he was comin' back, Lord Tavish did?"

Luke was mesmerized by how the man's mouth barely moved when he spoke, though when he smiled after Luke nodded, he was sure he knew why. The blackened and chipped teeth had to hurt like hell. It would have taken years of neglect or some powerful blows to get them to such an extreme.

"Well, if'n he did tell ye such, then he'll be 'ere. Otherwise..." He let his gaze rake down Luke from head to toe and then threw his head back and laughed at the scowl he received. "If not, I'll be back to take ye to hell." With another deep laugh, he turned back to the door, unbolted it and pulled the round ring to let himself in.

The moans and screams mixed with the repugnant smell that wafted out before the door closed had Luke stumbling back toward the dirt wall of his cell, his hands covering his nose. He'd always thought castle dungeons were part of the myth and folklore. *You always thought time travel was impossible, too.* He rolled his eyes at the voice in his head and slid back down to the floor to wait for his release.

Back against the wall, elbows on bent knees, he exhaled into his hands as he scrubbed them down his face. Keeping one ear alert for the sounds of the door above opening, Luke let his exhausted mind wander. None of this was truly possible. Was it?

His eyes scanned the room and thought about the door at the top of the steps. Just a few days ago, he and his youngest brother had found that door. At least he thought it was the same door. Set into one of the remaining walls of Somerled Keep, covered by at least a century of overgrown vegetation, the door would have remained hidden had Will not stumbled. The bush, followed by an unmistakable metal thud, had broken his brother's fall and had the two men pulling back the vegetation to see what they had found. Luke had expected armor or some kind of artwork. He definitely wouldn't have considered a door. He tried to remember the layout of the old castle ruins, wracking his brain for what he'd expected to find on the other side. Certainly, not steps carved into the dirt beneath the castle leading into a dungeon.

Together, he and Will had tried to pry off the locks that had been added to the thick, wooden plank that stretched across the door and fit snuggly into cradles on either side. They'd managed to break one, but the years and the elements had other plans. Luke told Will they'd come back with the proper tools to get the job done. The twenty-four-year-old had shrugged, putting his palm against the door one more time before turning to finish their rounds about the old ruins. His brows drawn, Luke had stared at the door, putting his palm against it as well before quickly stepping away. The door, even in the cool of the morning, was warm to the touch. He'd made a mental note to ask his great grandfather about the door... a note that he never got around to pulling back out again.

Three days later, he and Mairi were up checking the ruins after Will hadn't come home and she'd wanted them to go down there. *Mairi.* The thought of the foul-mouthed girl, who seemed to have always been a part of their lives, made Luke smile. Sexy as sin... at least the woman she was growing up to be was. She'd been a bit homely as a young girl and early teenager, but she'd recently grown into her big blue eyes that she swore were a dark shade of purple. And that sandy brown hair that looked red in the sunlight... It had *run your fingers through it while you kiss me hard up against a wall* woven into every strand. Too bad he'd never get to do that.

Mairi had the hots for his older brother, Seth. At thirty-one, Seth had to be what... thirteen years older than her? Luke shook his head, wondering if she even remembered Seth or if it was just the memory of him that had her teenage body all wet and ready. He'd joined the military when she was just ten and hadn't returned until she was fourteen. After that, he'd been back every two years. Maybe. It made no sense to him why she'd taken such a liking to Seth. He would have been better suited for her. Or Will. Luke sighed. Truthfully, Mairi and Will would have made the better match. They were closer in age, though Will was probably too much of a dreamer for Mairi. Maybe not. She loved her old jewelry and ancient artifacts and often looked like she was walking back in time when she'd talk about them. That was close to day dreaming.

Time. Walking back in time... Luke let himself think of the woman he'd seen just before... He shook his head. This was crazy. There had to be another explanation. Maybe he'd been hit in the head when he and Mairi had moved the debris away from the metal door and it had flown open with the gush of foul-smelling air that blew out from inside. He squinted, remembering the two of them fighting the door closed and working the thick wooden bar back over it. After a few minutes of startled laughter, they'd made their way back toward the front of Somerled where they'd encountered the woman. What had she said her name was? He wracked his brain.

Amileigh. Amileigh McCollum, she'd said. The only daughter of Gairlich McCollum. He searched his mind, trying to remember the history of the old castle, though history had never really been his cup of tea. If he wasn't mistaken, Gairlich McCollum and his family had lived in the Keep around... six hundred years ago. Luke groaned. Maybe this was all just a really bad joke.

But the fully restored Keep hadn't been a joke, though. He'd dived across dirt and grass in the midst of ruins to keep the woman from hitting her head on jutting debris when she fell, and landed with his hands beneath her, both of their bodies sprawled on cool tile within a warm, fully enclosed entry hall fit for a castle.

God, his head hurt. And that damn humming... When had that started? He thought... when he'd rounded the corner of the crumbling entryway. No. Before that. He'd been dealing with a slight hum ever since his hand had contacted the metal door that first time, only he'd pushed it aside, figuring it was a change in the weather or whatever shift was occurring that was causing the earth tremors. By the time he'd entered the entryway area of the old Keep, the sound in his head had grown to the point he'd had to really fight against it to concentrate on the woman. What did he remember of her between the time he'd first seen her in the future and been pulled away from her in the past? Or would that be present? Luke didn't really care. All of it made his brain hurt, especially since thoughts of her seemed to be causing the hum to grow.

Crazy, he thought. That was how he felt about the situation as well as what he'd thought when he first saw the woman who claimed she was Amileigh McCollum. Stunning, but batshit crazy in her long, creamy-white dress covered in dirt and dried leaves. Other than being soiled, the dress looked like something Mairi might have had in the little antiques and vintage clothing store she ran with his great grandmother. The woman's long, blonde hair was obviously thick given by the width of the braid draped over her shoulder. It was probably beautiful when it was loose and clean. But the way she'd held herself, as if life itself was confusing and terrifying... except when she looked at him.

When her eyes locked with his, he'd wanted to make the world stop for her, forcing it to answer all her unasked questions, and she'd looked at him as if she believed he could do it. He'd been unable to tear his gaze away from her from that point on, especially when she practically licked her lips when she was looking him over. Luke was certain he'd laughed at that, or at least smirked. It wasn't like it was a response he'd never had from women. He and his brothers were all decent looking men, naturally fit. He also spent a fair amount of time defining in his home gym and he supposed his line of work helped too. He'd always dreamed of restoring old houses, and that's what he'd ended up doing after his college years. His great grandfather had laughed when he'd first told him what he wanted to do, which really didn't make sense, especially with the old man's love of history and freakishly guardian-like concern over Somerled.

Beyond that, Luke wasn't entirely sure exactly what Kiernan did since he was already retired by the time Luke met him for the first time. Now Kiernan mostly puttered around, pestering his grandmother and Mairi at the antiques shop, and pushing Luke and his brothers to make sure they settled close to Ruthven Manor. At least he was when he wasn't off traveling somewhere, which he also seemed to do a lot.

Luke groaned again. So much of his life was starting to make sense and yet still made no sense at all. He let his head fall back against the wall behind him. Where was Kiernan? And where was the woman? Amileigh.

Chapter 5

Kiernan practically burst through Gairlich's study door after running all the way up the steps from the holding cell and back to the wing where the man waited. Gairlich jumped when the door flew open and Kiernan spent the first few seconds apologizing to the Lord of Somerled.

"Well?" Gairlich commanded, his tone holding irritation that Kiernan suspected went well beyond the irreverent intrusion.

"Aye, my Lord. I do believe this man is from the future. Some nearly 600 years, to be exact," Kiernan told him through labored breaths. At Gairlich's urging, Kiernan told him what all had been said and about the coin, all the while, Gairlich sat at his desk staring down at a large book opened before him.

"Stop," Gairlich ordered at one point. "What did you say was his name?"

Kiernan told him and Gairlich nodded, spinning the book around and pushing it toward the opposite side of the massive desk.

Looking from the open page back to Gairlich, and then back at the book, Kiernan caressed the pages with reverence before asking, "Where did you get this?" When Gairlich didn't speak, Kiernan turned his eyes back to the somber man.

"You... you know what it is?"

Kiernan nodded. It was the book that mentioned Luke's name. Loukas, actually, but they were too similar to be coincidence.

Gairlich sighed. "It's been passed down from generation

to generation since the beginning... Saundra's mother, Lady Cairistine, told me I should entrust it to no one, save for my own daughter should I have one, or a woman named..." He closed his eyes for a moment, their confusion replaced with clarity when he opened them again. "She said someday I would meet a woman named Abra. Though that day has yet to come, and now my own daughter is about to be whisked away from me." Gairlich's voice rose and he slammed his fist down on his desk making the scattered contents jump along with his companion.

Kiernan sucked in a loud breath, knowing Gairlich probably thought his reaction was to his outburst. That had surprised him a little, though he might well have acted the same way. No, his surprise was that Abra, his Abra, had been named. The sacred tomes of the Nebrani were to be entrusted to his beloved, and if everything went as Fate seemed to be orchestrating, perhaps someday they would be returned to Amileigh. Just in a different time.

With a loud sigh, Gairlich reached over and pulled the book back in front of him where he set about wrapping it in a soft cloth before returning it to a locked cabinet behind his desk. "I should have paid more attention to the books. I've read through most of them. Though briefly. I just never imagined any of this would happen during my lifetime. Certainly, not to my daughter."

"I know Abra," Kiernan practically whispered.

Kiernan's confession had Gairlich straightening and turning toward him rather quickly, his bronze brows drawing down along with his mouth. "Do tell. You are a man of many secrets, Lord Tavish."

Kiernan chuckled. More than most of them would ever know. "Yes, though I believe our first line of action is to bring your daughter and the captive man face to face to see what happens. I have concerns that the Dubhagan have caught wind of your daughter's maturity and perhaps even Fate's plans. We would do well to take caution. Heaven forbid we stand in Fate's way."

Gairlich's lips thinned, his eyes dulling. He finally nodded. "I suppose we have no choice. I will summon her here. You go and fetch the man."

The knock on Amileigh's door had been expected and yet she still jumped. Abigail tittered, her laugh nervous and unsure as she finished tying the bow at her mistress' waist and stepped back. The smile on the young woman's face told Amileigh exactly what it always did... that she looked quite fetching. Her hair loose, she pulled it around to drape over one shoulder and smoothed the mass of curls before moving to open the door.

"Auley! I... I thought Kiernan was coming back to get me?" Amileigh looked past her brother, attempting to see if the other man was present. All she saw was a servant slipping away back down the hall.

Auley snorted. "Sorry, Sis. All you get is me." She rolled her eyes and he continued. "I am to escort you to Father's study at once. Not sure what you've gotten yourself into, but being called to the study is never good news." He laughed when she scoffed and swatted at the arm he held out for her. "Come on, Prissy Butt. You took so long answering the door that we need to hurry."

"I didn't take that long," she huffed at him and stepped into the hallway, her legs feeling suddenly heavy. Each step toward her father's study filled her with increasing dread. And yet there was an air of excitement as well. At least there was until she faced the man who had helped bring her into this world. His handsomely stern features etched with concern, he motioned for her to sit down in one of the oversized wingback chairs near the fireplace at the far end of the room.

"We need to talk…" her father began.

Auley was right. Those were never good words. Amileigh nodded, her head remaining down so that he could not see the tears forming in her eyes. With a deep breath, she turned away from his desk.

Several steps away from the chairs, she stopped, placing her fingertips against her temples and closing her eyes. The hum had suddenly increased to the point that she was no longer certain she would be able to move. Her father was at her side almost instantly. She could feel his strong arms around her as he helped her cross the final distance and sit down just before the door opened. Kiernan stepped in, followed by the man… the one she had seen in the ruins of Somerled.

The loud sucking in of Amileigh's breath had all eyes turning in her direction. She noticed only the man. She could feel nothing beyond the tenseness in her body and the unnerving desire to rise and go to him. He stared back as she looked him over, noting the peach rose colored shirt had been fastened and tucked into the strange britches. His dark hair, though she could tell he'd at least combed his fingers through it, still looked ruffled. She longed to touch it, to run her palm down the side of his face, to…

Lord, help me, she prayed silently. These were not thoughts a proper lady should be thinking. She watched him staring at her, wondering if his thoughts ran parallel to hers. His cold blue stare told her nothing. It only made her shiver.

Luke hadn't expected to see the woman when he'd entered the room, but there she was staring at him with eyes unlike any he'd ever seen. They were a lighter purple than Mairi's—if hers really were purple, this woman's eyes were hard to describe. They were almost translucent, and yet not. Regardless, they drew him in and he began to wonder if she was enchanted. Perhaps that's why the humming in his head had grown stronger with every step toward the room. He'd wanted to ask Kiernan about it, but the man had already told him all his questions would be answered in due time, that they just needed to hurry to the Lord's study, where he was waiting for them.

When Kiernan had first come to get him, Luke had half expected to emerge through the metal door to find it had all been a ruse, some joke played on him by his brother or Mairi, but that hadn't been the case. They'd climbed the steps and gone through the doorway into a fully restored Somerled that had his mouth dropping open as they walked through the grand halls toward the place where he'd first seen the woman and on toward Lord McCollum's study.

Though there were still signs of finery to be seen, he would never have guessed just how wealthy the family must have been to have afforded such lavish materials. The craftsman who had designed the banister alone must have cost a small fortune. Now *this* was a project he'd love to take on someday... restoring an old castle to its former glory.

Luke looked at Kiernan's back, watched him as they walked toward their destination. If he truly was his great grandfather... which still seemed impossible given the time span, why had he not rebuilt the place? The Kiernan of Luke's time surely had to know what had happened. Luke frowned. If his great grandfather had known he would be thrust back in time, why had the old man not told him? Surely there had to be more than just telling him to keep a coin in his pocket. Shouldn't he have known the date and time?

An invisible current seemed to bring the hairs on the back of Luke's neck to a salute. There were too many unanswered questions. Too much that didn't add up, yet this Kiernan had told him his questions would be answered. Luke looked around again right before the hum grew to a deafening level, taking all his concentration. He guessed he'd have to wait to find out. Really, what other choice did he have?

When Kiernan had opened the study door and they'd stepped through, the hum was roaring so loudly in his head he couldn't hear what the Lord of the castle was saying to him. He probably wouldn't have listened anyway, his attention instead riveted to the young woman who sat in the chair beside where her father stood, his hand resting protectively on her shoulder. *Amileigh*. She heard it too— the hum. At least her fingers pressed to her temple made him believe she did. She'd looked him over again, much as she had in the ruins before she'd passed out and they'd hurled through time together. Of course, they'd end up in her time... but how had she found her way into his in the first place? And if he touched her again... was that the trigger? Is that what it would take to send him home?

When Luke rushed toward her, both Kiernan and her father quickly blocked his way.

"I... I'm sorry," he stammered, looking at the two men briefly before refocusing on the woman who had stood and moved behind the chair. "I just thought..." He sighed. "I'm tired. I just want to go home."

Kiernan nodded while pushing Luke back a step or two with a hand to his chest. "Keep your head, man. We've a lot to sort out here. Besides..." He looked over his shoulder then back again before continuing in a hushed voice, "I don't think that's the answer. I doubt merely touching her will be enough to create another ripple in time."

Luke was surprised Kiernan had so fully understood and even more surprised when Kiernan chuckled.

"That's not to say I don't believe she is the key to many of your unanswered questions, my young friend."

Frowning, Luke nodded slowly, though he was really thinking everyone around him was truly crazy. It wasn't until he felt the light pressure of a small hand against his arm that he realized Kiernan might just be right. Her touch hadn't blasted him through time. No angels sang, the heavens didn't open... but he felt a moment of peace like nothing he'd ever felt before. It was like being complete or coming home... everything right all rolled up into one.

And there was something else. As he looked down, through those lilac eyes into the soul of the woman standing next to him, something stirred inside him. Not the sexual stirrings of the suddenly starving man that he was... he had to admit everything in that department was firing on all cylinders. But this... this was something else, something he'd never felt before. It was a power apart from himself as if someone or some *thing* pressed to be released. A low growl formed in his throat and he forced himself to swallow it down.

"Easy." Kiernan's voice broke through the haze and Luke managed to tear his gaze away from the eyes that had stirred something inside.

Clearing his throat to garner their attention, the Lord of Somerled motioned toward a highbacked sofa against the wall behind them. "Sit," he told them. "We have much to discuss, and I'm guessing not a lot of time in which to do it." He looked at Kiernan who nodded and pulled a chair to where he was sitting before them once they sunk into the cushions, Amileigh's hand still on Luke's arm. It seemed... natural.

"Luke, Amileigh. I know this all seems a bit crazy. I'm not sure I understand it all myself. But... uh. This thing you're feeling." He pointed at where Amileigh's hand rested on Luke's arm. "And the whole traveling through time... It's obvious that your destinies were meant to collide. There's a whole lot more to it, but the best thing for you, for all of us really, would be if the two of you married immediately."

"What?!" Amileigh and Luke both answer at the same time.

"Are you mad?"

Kiernan had never seen Amileigh move so quickly, but the young maiden shot up from the sofa, moving around her father's desk, and stationing herself in front of the window with a speed that made his warrior blood proud.

"Look." The word pulled all eyes back to Luke. "I'm sorry." He was looking at Amileigh. "You're a lovely girl. Really. And I'm sure you'll make the right man a great wife, but I'm not interested in marrying anyone." He stood up, an action that was mirrored by Kiernan. "I just want to get out of here and go home. There has to be a way."

Kiernan stepped in Luke's way as he turned toward the door. "What you're not understanding is that without this union our kind will die. The Dubhagan will come for the girl... they are already trying. Eventually, they will win, and life as we know it will be no more." He sighed loudly. "I can't fight this battle alone, Luke. I need you." He paused and turned to Amileigh. "And you."

No one spoke for several seconds though it was obvious the wheels of thought were turning. It was Luke who first broke the silence.

"What do you mean *our kind*?"

Kiernan chewed on his lower lip before breathing in a deep breath and blowing it out. "Locked away inside you, Luke, is a... dragon." Kiernan put his hand up to still the scoffs of disbelief from both Amileigh and Luke. "Hear me out. Over a thousand years ago, when dragons freely roamed the earth, one band became power hungry. They didn't want to be equal to man, they wanted to rule them, to enslave them as their providers."

"Much like many of the lords and serfs of today." Amileigh's soft words floated across the room.

Kiernan nodded. "Somewhat, only much more menacing." He turned back to Luke. "Great slaying parties ensued and both the friendlier Kedan and the darker Dubhagan dragons were being killed. One clan of people saw the detriment to the extinction and stepped in, making a pact with the King of the Dragons of Kedan. These people, the Nebrani, held a certain... magic." Kiernan paused again, letting his words settle in for a few seconds. "The Nebrani Wizards concocted a serum that infused the essence of the Kedan dragons into men deemed to possess great courage and valor. However, it took the power of certain Nebrani women to make it all happen. Those women, Prihoms or Keys, were required to unlock the dragons inside these men."

"How?" Luke interrupted. "This is insane. But if it was true, how do these *magical* women get these dragons out of the infused men?"

Luke squirmed, pulling at his shirtfront before rubbing the back of his hand with his palm. Kiernan smiled. *You feel it, don't you? The great beast inside you is straining to be set free, waiting for you to acknowledge him.*

"They don't *get out*, Luke. You...you shift from man to dragon." Kiernan watched his face closely for understanding. "But that won't happen, can't happen until...until you're ma...mated with a Prihom. Preferably *your* Prihom. Your Key."

Kiernan turned to Amileigh and both men watched her father move closer to her. All the color, what little there was, had drained from her face.

"I'm not going to try to fully explain all of this now, and I won't pretend to understand why you were brought back in time. I do know I've been searching for other Kedan Blends for years to no avail. Maybe there are none left." He shrugged. "I also know nothing about what is happening in your world now, Luke. I'm not sure why you were sent back. So, I don't have all the answers. I can tell you Amileigh is from the purest of pure Prihoms. She's also obviously reached maturity as a Key, which is why the Dubhagan are now searching for her."

Amileigh sunk into her father's desk chair. "The shadows... they were these dragons you speak of?"

Kiernan nodded.

"So, wait." Luke's voice was edged with the same skepticism as his stance. He was looking at Amileigh. "You mean to tell me you're buying into all this? You believe..." He scoffed. "You've *seen* these dragons?"

Amileigh looked from Luke to Kiernan and waited a few seconds before nodding. "I've been seeing the shadows for a while now. A couple of weeks. Maybe a month. But right before... Kiernan and I had ridden out to enjoy a picnic Mother had had prepared for us, only as we rode, there was a sound of great mayhem behind us. Kiernan yelled at me to ride to the cave, to not look back. But I did. I turned around and saw the great beasts, three of them, hideous creatures chasing another." Her expression softened, a sweet smile playing over her mouth. "That one was beautiful, his colors vibrant, his eyes..." She looked at Kiernan. "His eyes were a deep, dark crystal blue and they were filled with great care and concern."

She looked back at Luke and winced at the single eyebrow he had inched above the other. She thinned her lips and strengthened her resolve. His dislike for her was obvious and Prihom or not, she'd not allow herself to be used by some man who cared nothing for her.

"I need to lie down, Father," she told him while pushing herself away from the desk. "I'm not feeling well."

Gairlich McCollum took his daughter's arm, his hand going to her back. "Of course, my love. This has undoubtedly been a great shock to you. To all of us, really." He looked at the two men. "I'll escort her to her room. Just wait for me here."

Kiernan nodded and Luke followed suite. Just like he'd thought earlier, what else could he do? As a man in a time not his own, he was rather at the mercy of his "hosts." He'd have to ride this out, try to figure out his options. He watched the girl walk past, caught scent of her fresh apple cranberry fragrance, and noticed for the first time that the humming sound had simmered to a more bearable ringing in his ears. He squinted, realizing things had changed from the moment she'd laid her hand on his arm and he'd covered it with his own. He could feel that odd stirring inside again, felt it reaching out to her as she walked by. Did she feel it too? Is that why her lilac eyes grew wide?

He smiled, a small gesture, just before she looked away and went through the door. *She's stalling, looking for answers just like you.* Luke wished he could silence that inner voice, the one that had been with him always, as far as he could remember.

"I'm not stalling," he mumbled under his breath. "At least not anymore." He turned back to Kiernan. "So, what else do I need to know?"

Kiernan pointed to the sofa and both men sat back down.

Amileigh could feel her whole body shaking as her father escorted her back to her room. He'd already dispatched a servant to make sure Abigail was there waiting for her.

"What will you tell Mother?" she asked, hating the feathery quietness of her voice. She felt her father tense, knew a talk with her mother was not something he was looking forward to. "You could send her to me."

Gairlich's greying blonde topped head shook. "And have her take matters into her own hands? Nay. Let us work this out through Kiernan first."

Amileigh nodded, kissing her father's cheek at her doorway when he pulled her into a tight hug. "I don't wish to marry him, Father. I don't know him and there's no way he could have any feelings for me. The stranger, I mean."

Gairlich nodded as he pulled away, though his eyes and smile were both sad. "We all do things we don't want to do, love. But perhaps there is another way." He patted the cheek of his only daughter and turned to walk away.

"Perhaps," she whispered. Her mind went to Kiernan. Why could he not marry her? She thought of the beautiful winged creature with Kiernan's eyes. If he could already transform, did that mean... She refused to let herself think of

Kiernan enraptured with another. She couldn't fathom it any more than she could see herself with Luke.

Tendrils of heat spread inside her. Maybe she could see it. Maybe she just didn't want to. Amileigh opened her door just in time to see the shadow fall away from her window.

Chapter 6

Back down in Gairlich's study, Kiernan had tried to explain a few things while they waited for the castle lord to return. He'd hoped Luke would understand and be ready to discuss plans for a hasty marriage between himself and Amileigh when Gairlich returned. The whole thing was unconventional and would take some coercion to bend the laws of the land to seeing things their way. It wasn't like they could waltz in and tell the truth. The reality was, they would keep everything as hushed as possible, but the walls always talked. He hated that, felt his gut clench at having to make Amileigh go through this. As sweet as she was, there was no way her reputation would not be soiled. He only hoped by her going ahead and marrying the handsome stranger, society would somehow overlook what they would believe as her indiscretions. Try as he might, Kiernan could see no other way.

"So, let me get this straight. We get married, there's something about this ceremony that unlocks my powers, and I turn into a dragon?" The disbelief was thick in Luke's voice but he hadn't bolted yet. Kiernan was appreciative of that.

"Something like that. It's more the uhm… actual mating that completes your transformation and allows *you* to shift into dragon form." Kiernan waited for Luke to respond, waving his hand in front of the man's face when he didn't.

Luke jumped, blinked a few times, and then began to laugh. "Oh, this is rich." He looked at Kiernan and smiled. "Technically, I don't have to *marry* her I just have to *sleep* with her." He waggled his eyebrows at Kiernan who now openly glared back.

Holding his breath for a second, Kiernan scrubbed his hands down his face and sat back. "Technically," Kiernan tried out the odd word, "one would hope there would not be a lot of sleeping that occurred, but…"

Clapping his hands, Luke jumped up and walked over to the window. "This is going to be a piece of cake," he mumbled to himself. He'd just have sex with the girl and go home.

As he breathed in, Amileigh's lingering scent tickled his senses and Luke noticed his heart pitching just a bit. He frowned. Let's not get carried away, he told himself. She's only here long enough to let me unlock this dragon. And if that turns out to be some kind of lie, well, at least we're not saddled with her forever. Really, she didn't fit his taste in women at all. It wasn't that she was bad looking or anything. Truth be told, she was downright beautiful. Just not what he was usually attracted to. If the twitching below his belt was any indication, there was some definite attraction there. Maybe it was just because it had been a while since he'd been with anyone. It wasn't like he wasn't needy.

He shifted and huffed. In an attempt to get his mind off the two of them tangled together between the sheets, Luke tried to concentrate on the supposed dragon that lived inside of him.

Not in you. As part of you. I'm in your blood, your bones, in every cell of your body.

Startled by the boldness of the voice, Luke turned around to stare at Kiernan. He'd always heard a voice, just not so forcefully. Had it always been the beast inside?

Swallowing, he cleared his throat. "So, he began before moving back toward the sofa, "how exactly does all this dragon shifting stuff work anyway?"

Kiernan shook his head, the hope in his eyes dulled. "You'll not get past her father with thoughts like that. I don't know how things are done in your time, but here... ladies are ladies, and this is going to be difficult enough for the family to endure."

Luke crinkled his nose, his brows coming down. *Endure?* What the hell did they think *he* was having to do? Ripped from his own time-period, told he was a freakin' dragon, expected to marry some girl... If he did get back home, and he intended to do everything he could to do so, what would that mean? He'd have a wife some six hundred years in the past? Too damn bad. Luke marched over to the door, reaching for the handle just as it began to open. He stepped back to let a startled Gairlich through.

"I'm sorry, but..." He looked from Luke to Kiernan and back to Luke again, once he'd composed himself from the start. "My daughter has refused your offer of marriage and I'm obliged to agree with her." He turned to Kiernan again, ignoring Luke's raised brows and open mouth. "I'm sorry, Kiernan. There simply has to be another way."

Kiernan slumped against his chair, putting his face in his hands as he leaned over fighting for air. What he'd thought would be a reprieve for him... a step toward him having help to fight this battle and maintain the existence of the Kedan was turning into a complete disaster.

Don't give up. Move forward as if our plans were all falling into place. Nicholai's voice sounded in his head and Kiernan nodded before giving himself a mental shake and standing up.

"Gairlich, would you care greatly if this stranger borrowed some of Auley's clothing? And would you be so kind as to give the two of us lodging in your guest wing for a few nights?"

Somerled's Lord stared at the man who appeared to be just a few years older than his twins. Kiernan could see the questions clouding his vision.

Trust me. Kiernan smiled when Gairlich's slight nod indicated he understood the plea in Kiernan's eyes.

"My household is at your disposal. Just..." The Lord's eyes hardened when he looked at Luke. "Just stay away from my daughter."

With that, he stepped out of the doorway and waved his guests past.

Neither Kiernan or Luke acknowledged Gairlich's words, though if anyone could have read either of their minds, they would have known each of their thoughts mirrored the others. They were both absolutely certain his request was not going to be honored. Luke saw Amileigh as his ticket home. Kiernan knew the truth. Their union would take place, marriage or not. He thought of Abra and how nothing could keep the dragon at bay once his key had been found. Not customs, not fear, and certainly not the command of a father.

Luke wasn't surprised at the odd looks he got as he followed Kiernan through the halls of Somerled. He nodded, trying to size up the people, to see who he might eventually be able to consider someone willing to help him, all while trying to get his bearings. He'd spent enough time as a kid poking around the ruins of the old castle, and more with the upkeep in later years, that he felt like he should have known exactly where he was at all times. Only when they climbed the glamorous staircase and turned right instead of left, he was at a complete loss. This part of the house hadn't endured at all other than a portion of the hallway below, a few base walls, debris scattered here and there, and some steps at the far end of the first floor. Certainly, none of the structure from the second or third stories in this area had remained intact.

At the other end of the hall, the rooms could still be accessed by ladder, though they were in the process of building a period replica staircase along the back. The state, having long before deemed Somerled a historical site, had decided recently that tours of the old place should go beyond a walk through the grounds. Too many visitors had expressed a desire to be able to sample a taste of what it was like to have lived in an actual castle, and since Somerled was one of the few that had whole rooms still intact with rooms on the first two floors of the west wing still structurally sound... other than the second floor having no permanent access... the state had chosen it.

Just outside a set of opened, oversized wooden doors, Kiernan stopped to talk to a servant and Luke took the opportunity to look back down the hallway to where another set of doors flanked the beginning of the wing leading to the rooms that had remained intact in the future. He'd always suspected that section of the castle housed the family quarters. The wooden doors probably kept outsiders from unwanted intrusion when the house was full of guests. The last time he'd been up there he'd found a stash of empty beer bottles near a spot that would have been just beyond the doors—close to the place where they put the ladder to climb up. He suspected his brother Will since Somerled was far enough out that it didn't attract a lot of unwanted visitors, at least not during the night. He chuckled under his breath thinking how he and his brothers had all taken a girl or two up to the ruins to woo her in the moonlight among the mysterious walls. A lot of people thought the place was haunted. Looking around, Luke could almost believe those people had been right.

When the servant moved past him, Luke was startled out of his musings. Kiernan motioned for him to follow.

"I've sent her to fetch clothing from Auley," Kiernan told him when he turned to watch the woman disappear down the West hall. "I'll see you settled into your room."

"I'm guessing you spend a lot of time here," Luke said, still trying to get his bearings as they walked to the far end of the hall. "Where exactly do you live?"

Kiernan stopped, his hand reaching for the doorknob in front of him. He turned and stared at his companion and Luke had the feeling he was debating on whether or not he should answer. After a few seconds, he shrugged. "A short ride from here. In Tavish Manor." He opened the door and waited for Luke to follow him inside. "With my wife," he added as the door swung shut.

Luke nodded. "Abra?" Stepping back, Kiernan covered his heart with his hand before he nodded and Luke laughed. "She's my great grandmother, remember?"

"Of course," Kiernan laughed as well. "I just... I can't imagine our lives six hundred years from now. Is she... are we both well, then?"

Luke nodded. "You're a lot older, of course. In your eighties. At least that's what you look." He narrowed his eyes, squinting at the younger looking man. "Just how old are you anyway?"

Kiernan shuffled a bit and went to look out the window that wasn't a whole lot bigger than a cracker box. He took his time before he answered. "Three hundred and forty-two now, give or take a decade here and there." He laughed at the shock on Luke's face.

"So, that would make you what? Over nine hundred years old in my time?" Luke shook his head. "I just don't see..."

"Nothing to see," Kiernan interrupted. "Once you're transformed, you and your mate have the ability to live forever, at least if you can escape being killed or barring you contract some incurable illness. The later isn't that likely. Dragon Blends don't seem to be inflicted the same as humans."

Luke thought for a moment then nodded. "So, how many are there... dragon Blends, I mean? And their mates, too."

Kiernan sighed and looked down at his feet, beginning to toe an imaginary spot on the carpet. "None that I'm aware of. Kedan Blends, that is. I can't sense all Prihoms, so I don't know the answer to that. In fact, other Prihoms can't always sense their own kind. But if we're still and quiet long enough, we can usually tell when others of our own species are around, whether they're transformed or not." He looked up at Luke. "Obviously, my offspring would have the ability to be either, though I currently have only daughters, and since Abra is a Prihom and I am a Blend, they would not be considered as pure as someone like Amileigh."

Luke chewed on the inside of his cheek. "And she's considered pure because? Other than not having... you know." He looked back when Kiernan chuckled.

"Her grandmothers on both sides are Prihom, and their husbands both descended from Prihom blood. Since Gairlich's mother is Prihom and his father is from Prihom lineage, even though he is male, Gairlich is considered of pure blood as well. That makes Amileigh the purest of pure."

Both men looked up as a strange shadow blocked the sun from the window that wasn't much bigger than a man's boot box. Kiernan's brows were drawn when he looked back at Luke. "And very desirable to many. Now, if you'll excuse me, I need to speak to Gairlich again. I think an extra guard might be a good idea for his daughter."

Luke waited for Kiernan to leave before walking over to the window. He wasn't sure what the odd shadow had been, though he'd felt a strange prickling at the back of his neck just before it had darkened the window. He looked out but could see nothing anywhere nearby. He shook his head. It was the fourteen hundreds, not like there would have been any sort of flying machines around during that time. At least he couldn't remember any mentioned in his history classes. He chuckled. Of course, they hadn't mentioned dragons, and certainly not dragon shifters, either.

Turning away from the window, he leaned against the wall. Man, he was tired. He massaged his temples. For some reason, the hum had begun to grow louder again. He looked at the bed. Maybe a few minutes of shuteye would help. When Kiernan returned, he'd surely hear him.

Untucking his shirt, he unbuttoned it and dragged it off to drape across one of the chairs. He looked around. The room wasn't huge, but it wasn't exactly small either. He'd say it was probably equivalent to most master bedrooms in some of the nicer houses he'd helped build or restore. Not bad for a guest room, especially since it was obviously one of many. He reached down to unlace his work boots, and after toeing them off, climbed up on the bed. It wasn't the softest mattress he'd ever felt, but it would do.

After picking away the end of a feather or two that poked through the linens on the pillow, he fluffed it up and balled it under his head. Good or not, it felt like heaven as he drifted into a sleep so sound it would have taken God himself to have awakened him... Or the touch of an angel.

Luke's dreams were filled with a cranberry rose scent and an angel with long, blonde curls nestled against ivory cheeks, her lilac eyes luring him closer. She smiled at him, and it wasn't until he reached for her and pulled her over him that his eyes popped open to find Amileigh squirming in his arms.

"Unhand me!"

Luke stared at her, his forehead crinkling in confusion for several seconds before he twisted, landing her on the bed beside where he'd been, his hands on either side of her. Looking down, he raised his brows, laughing as she tried to push herself further into the bedding to distance herself from him.

"Let me go," she demanded again.

"Or?" He bent his arms slightly, bringing him closer to the blonde angel.

"Or, I'll scream!"

Luke shook his head. "I don't think so." He laughed when she started to position her hands against his bare chest to push herself away, then thought better of it. "You wouldn't want anyone to see you in here alone with me." His smile widened when she scrunched her nose and scoffed, but he could see the truth in her lilac eyes. Yes, he remembered enough about history and those damn romance novels Mairi was always telling him about to know just being in a room alone with a man was enough to ruin her reputation. Not that it mattered. It was going to get ruined soon enough.

He made the mistake of looking down at her mouth. Damn, he thought snuggling in closer to her. Damn if she didn't feel good in his arms. Almost perfect. Damn, damn, damn.

Without thought, he closed the distance between them, his mouth locking over hers.

Amileigh hadn't bargained for a tousle when she'd rapped on the door to no response before sneaking into the stranger's bedroom. When she'd seen him sleeping, curled on his side wearing nothing but the odd pants, she should have closed the door and ran as fast as she could back to her own room. But she hadn't. Instead, she'd tiptoed up beside the large bed, her head urging her to touch him. Just one feel. That's all. Just enough to confirm that he was real.

Only when her fingers had made contact with his warm skin, she ran her palm down his arm, feeling the hard planes beneath her hand. She'd sighed and stopped to trace some of the *ink* that covered his lower forearm. What was it? A tail? Maybe... she looked at his chest. Maybe a dragon's tail. He'd moaned then, and she'd pulled her hand away, though not quickly enough. He reached out and grabbed her, pulling her atop him, her chest smashed against his.

She'd railed him with her words and he'd just laughed, at least he had after he'd tossed her on the bed and hovered above her like the prey animal he was. So why then did she feel as if she was the one starving and ready to eat him alive, every nerve in her body strumming and tensed while she waited for him to make his move?

When he lowered his mouth to hers, Amileigh wasn't

sure if she'd explode or dissolve into a fit of tears. Her instincts told her to push him away, to run, but her body had other ideas. Her nipples peaked, pressing toward him beneath the thin fabric of her gown, and the pressure growing between her legs… she'd never experienced anything quite like it. Not even the statues in the King's garden and her fantasies around them could compare.

"S…S… Stop," she whispered. It was a weak request when he pulled away and they both gulped air. And then she found her hands in his hair, urging his mouth back to hers when it seemed he might oblige. Lord help her, she thought. If he stopped, she was quite certain, without a doubt, that she would surely die.

"What the hell?!"

The familiar voice had the effect of a bucket of cold water being thrown over her and Amileigh rolled off the side of the bed just as the stranger rolled the other direction.

Breathing heavily, Amileigh began to stammer. "Ki… Oh, Kiernan. It's. It's n…not what it looks like. We were just…" Looking from her old friend to the stranger who stared at her with a lopsided grin, Amileigh covered her flaming cheeks with her hands and turned, running past Kiernan and out of the room.

Kiernan stepped into the hallway, staring after Amileigh's retreating back before turning to look in at Luke who was shrugging back into his shirt.

"I need to go talk to her." His glare was lost on his great grandson who was reaching down to gather his socks. "You! You need to stay put. And don't let anyone past this door!"

Falling into one of the armchairs, Luke stared at the door, the slam of it still ringing in his ears. Five more minutes and he'd have had her. Hell, his hand had already been working to find its way beneath that damned skirt. He reached down to adjust himself, but knew that would do nothing to alleviate his discomfort. What had he said about her not being his type? His rock-hard cock sure thought differently. If he closed his eyes, he could almost imagine...

Stop it, Luke! What was he doing? He wasn't some sixteen-year-old willing to blow his wad in his underwear over some girl just because he'd failed to get across home plate.

Amileigh almost had the lock secured when Kiernan pushed through her bedroom door.

"Go away!" she yelled at him as she flung herself across the bed, burying her face in the thick, white fabric.

Kiernan's heart broke as he watched her body shake and listened to her sobs. "Ami, I'm sorry. I should never have left him alone."

After several seconds of shuddering breaths, Amileigh finally pushed herself up and turned her tear-stained face toward her old friend. "It was me. I went to him." Fresh tears steaked down her face. "Oh, Kiernan. What's happening to me? What's going on."

With her eyes pleading with him, Kiernan felt his resolve weaken. He glanced out into the hall before stepping in to close the door and moving to where she had scooted to the edge of the bed. He dropped to the floor and took her hands in his trying to figure out where to start. After so many years of parenting, and especially having fathered his share of girls, one would think he would be better suited to handle these situations, but Kiernan had no idea where to start.

"I..." He was saved by Amileigh's interruption.

"When I turned eighteen, old Lord Ralleinsford asked for my hand. Do you remember, Kiernan? He would have been considered a great match, with all his lands and wealth. He held the King's favor as well."

The chip in Kiernan's heart widened along with her sad smile.

"I told father I would do it if he commanded it, but that I didn't want to. I wanted to wait for love, and he agreed, telling me he would never force me into a marriage." She sighed. "Only no other suitors came. It was as if all the young men had disappeared until I was twenty-one and Batair Draghan showed up." When she shivered, Kiernan rubbed her arm and she patted his hand. "I can't believe I almost fell for him."

They both nodded, though there was no way Kiernan could ever tell her the truth about Batair, that he belonged to the Dubhagan band and had only wanted to find out if she had the ability to unlock his dragon. It had taken some clever orchestration, but Kiernan had finally been able to show her Batair's true colors. He knew now that the vision of him with the young woman from Ellinias Castle still haunted Amileigh. How could it not when it was undoubtedly her first broken heart.

"This man," she continued, "I don't understand. I know he feels nothing for me and yet... I went to him, Kiernan. I allowed him to... to kiss me, to touch me..." New tears welled in her eyes. "I wanted him, like I have never wanted anyone in all my life. And yet... where is the love?"

Kiernan pushed himself up and wrapped his arms around her. "I'm sorry, Ami. I'm afraid it's the magic. It's deep inside of you, and inside of him, calling to one another. It's not conventional. Nothing about dragon Blends and their Prihom is." With a finger beneath her chin, he lifted her face up. "In time, your hearts would meld and you would learn to love him."

With a snort, Ami pushed away, grabbing a cloth to dry her tears. "You're just like Auley. Neither of you will ever understand." Standing up, she walked over and opened the door. "Just go." She refused to look at him as he filed by. "And tell that man to stay away from me. Next time, I will scream, regardless, and we'll see how he likes finding himself back in the dungeon."

Kiernan slowed his steps wondering if he should tell her about the shadows and what they truly were. The fact was, if she didn't mate with Luke, it was only a matter of time before the Dubhagan found a way to get her. If she was concerned about finding love, he wondered what she would think of ending up with a man who could barely claim he had a beating heart. At least not one that was capable of love.

He shook his head. That would have to wait until later. The guard had finally arrived and he needed to school him on what was needed to keep Amileigh safe, barring they lock her in her room, which he knew would raise the roof of the old castle. As long as she stayed inside and no one outside of himself and family was allowed near her, surely everything would be all right.

Had Kiernan seen the cloaked figure slip out of Amileigh's room while he and the guard were deep in discussion, he surely would have thought differently. Dressed in a light, golden-colored fall cloak, Amileigh marched down the hall and skipped down the back stairs. She even managed to steal through the kitchens without so much as a raised brow or a wary eye. It wasn't until she was three quarters of the way across the lawn and the dark shadow fell over her that she finally had to question the sanity of setting foot outside the walls and security of Somerled castle.

With one last glance at Amileigh's closed bedroom door, Kiernan fought the urge to go back inside and tell her exactly why she needed to reconsider. With a shrug, he turned back toward the rooms in the East wing attached to the landing on the far end of this hall. It was probably better to let her calm down. Perhaps then she'd be more open to logic.

Love, he thought with a chuckle just before opening the door to Luke's room. If that was all...

"I'm not going to apologize." Luke stood up as Kiernan walked through the door.

Kiernan leveled a stern glare at the other man. "I'm not asking you to, though it might behoove you to use your head... if you want to keep it. Regardless of the final outcome that we both know is necessary, she's still the daughter of the Lord of this castle. He's not going to take lightly you ravaging his daughter against her will."

Luke scoffed. "Against her will? Hell! She's the one who practically accosted me while I was sleeping."

With a humorless chuckle, Kiernan shook his head. "Twasn't her I saw on top of you when I walked in, lad."

Without answering, Luke turned away and walked over to the window wondering why the hairs on the back of his neck stood up again as he did. He didn't have to wait long for his answer as the dark shadow again fell over his window. Only this time, he got a good look at what was making it. He looked at Kiernan who had somehow materialized at his side.

Both men watched the black beast swoop toward a tiny figure at the edge of the forest. She tripped and the dragon pulled up to keep from hitting the trees. When she rose and her hood fell away, both men sucked in. It was Amileigh. They watched as she made another run for the forest.

"Good Lord," Kiernan whispered, already turning for the door.

Luke was only a few steps behind him, glad he'd already put his shoes back on.

As they ran down the hall, Kiernan grabbed a sword off the wall and tossed it to him while unsheathing his own. Luke barely caught it without it slicing into his hands and quickly resituated it so that his palm wrapped around the hilt. He stared down at it. What the hell was he supposed to do with it now?

"You'll know," Kiernan called back over his shoulder and motioned for Luke to follow. "It's in your blood. You're a warrior as well as a dragon."

Warrior, dragon, blood or no, Luke had his doubts, but he took the stairs two at a time on the heels of his great grandfather. He'd been in enough fights to know not to question, just do. For the most part, he'd come out the victor. Of course, he'd never fought a dragon before. Then again, he'd never fought for the woman he loved before either.

Chapter 7

Her chest heaving from the exertion, Amileigh zagged through the forest with one goal in mind, and that was getting to the security of the cave. She knew if she could get inside, the likelihood was small that the man who had replaced the dragon chasing her would even find the entrance. And if he did, there were plenty of hiding places inside.

Kiernan, she thought. Find me. *Not Kiernan, Luke... call for Luke.* The voice in her head startled Amileigh and she stumbled, regaining her footing just before she went down. She hurried on, refusing to call out for the strange man, though she was surprised that just thinking about him had set the noise in her head to humming again.

Luke looked up as they cleared the front entrance of the castle, surprised there was no black beast to be seen. Knowing the creature could not have flown through the dense forest, he'd expected to see it above their tops or flying over Somerled because surely Amileigh would circle around in an attempt to get back inside. At least that was what he would have done. Kiernan ran toward the trees at the far edge of the property. It was obvious he didn't believe so.

"Where are we going?" Luke yelled at him as he trudged along behind, sword in hand.

"To the cave. It's where she'll go."

He seemed so certain. Luke squinted and looked up at

the open sky above them one more time before it was obscured from view by the trees. Where the hell was that damned dragon?

By the time Kiernan slowed and lifted his hand to assure his partner proceeded quietly, Luke had just about decided they were on a wild goose chase. Had there even been a dragon, or had he imagined the whole thing? Hell, maybe there hadn't even been a girl. The way his cock twitched told him he knew the truth where she was concerned. He stopped completely when Kiernan motioned with his finger and both men froze seeing another figure in the distance before them.

"The girl?" he mouthed, knowing the answer even before Kiernan shook his head. Much larger than Amileigh, the figure appeared to have dark hair and was dressed in black clothing from what he could tell. He noticed the hair standing up on the back of his neck, much like it had when he'd seen the shadows earlier. Again, with his hand, Kiernan motioned for Luke to go in a direction that would take them away from the shadowy figure.

A fair distance away, Kiernan told Luke how far to go before circling around to look for the opening to the cave. He told him he would meet them there. Nodding, Luke stepped away, glad that his years of restoring old houses had given him at least an ability for judging distance.

Keeping an eye out for the landmarks Kiernan had given him, Luke still had trouble finding the entrance to the cave. What the hell did a three-trunk tree look like anyway? Frustrated, he stopped, and then it hit him. The humming in his head had grown louder the further he'd moved away from the edge of the shallow stream Kiernan had told him to follow part of the way. He had to be close. *She* had to be close.

He looked for the specific rock formation and nearly

missed it because of several overgrown trees. When he looked up, he noticed one of them sprouted up, forking into three rather large and distinct trunks. He smiled, knowing that hidden in the brush behind them was a small opening that would lead down into a cavern-like hallway that would take him to the cave. He closed his eyes for a moment before heading in and smiled again. The girl was there, waiting. And if Luke was quiet enough, he could almost hear her calling to him. He scrunched his forehead and shrugged. He knew that wasn't possible, but finding her safe and being able to hold her in his arms again... both of those were completely within his grasp.

Letting his eyes adjust for a few seconds, Luke made his way down the gentle slope, stopping every several feet to listen. He thought he heard the sounds of water somewhere in the distance, but he still saw nothing but darkness around him. Kiernan had told him natural light from a side opening above cascaded into the main chamber of the cave and that he'd be able to see it when he got close. The humming in his head remained about as loud as it had outside the cave, and he began to wonder if Amileigh was moving away from him. He closed his eyes and thought. *Where are you?* He waited, and just before he began to move again, her voice rang out.

Luke?

Luke stopped and looked around, surprised at how well his eyes had adjusted to the dark. But she wasn't nearby. The voice hadn't been audible. It had been inside his head.

Ami, Luke thought. He wasn't sure why he used the nickname he'd heard Kiernan use, but it felt right. *Wait. Kiernan sent me to find you. He said to have you take me to the Room of Embers and he'd meet us there. Can you... would you please wait or come to find me?*

When she didn't answer, he started to walk forward again. If she wouldn't cooperate, he'd just have to find her. He smiled, listening for the hum, pleased when it began to grow slightly louder. He doubted she was coming toward him, but her pace wasn't nearly as fast moving as it had been. She had to know he was gaining on her. A tremor shivered through him at the thought of being alone with her again. He wondered how Kiernan was fairing against Amileigh's pursuer and how long it would be before he joined them.

Amileigh huddled lower among the rocks. She'd heard the footsteps in the distance and wondered if she should remain in her hiding place or step out to intercept him. She knew it was Luke, had sensed him and heard the hum, most likely since before he'd entered the mouth of the cave. Now it was almost a dull roar so he had to know he was close to her. She tried to stand, though the intensity pushed against her and she stumbled back, sitting hard against the rock ledge in the tiny alcove. It reminded her of something within one of the day rooms back at Somerled and she wondered briefly whether this was where they got the idea. Not that it mattered. Right now, the hum and Luke were quickly taking over all thought.

"Luke," she called out when the pressure let up and she sensed he was moving away from her. Her heart beat against the bodice of her dress in anticipation of being found. Amileigh tried to push herself up. She shouldn't have waited. She should have gone to find him. She closed her eyes, the sounds inside her causing her head to swim, and when she opened them again, he was there, his face just inches away from hers in the dark. He knelt before moving forward, pressing himself between her knees as he cupped her face in his hands.

"Are you all right? That man... he didn't... he didn't hurt you, did he?"

Ami shook her head, his palms caressing her cheeks as she did. "He's one of them, you know. The Dubhagan."

Luke nodded though he looked like he didn't fully understand. Even in the dark, she could see his facial expressions. Or maybe she could sense them. She didn't know and it didn't matter. What mattered was he was there now, with her, and they were both safe. She looked at the sword Luke had laid on the rocks beside him.

"Where's Kiernan?"

"He'll be here. He's taking care of... some business."

Ami nodded, knowing exactly what sort of business. She was no stranger to this world of men and swords.

"I have to admit, I was damned afraid for you when I saw the dragon..."

When Ami nodded again and reached out to touch his cheek, Luke practically hissed. He pushed closer, her bunched up skirt the only thing protecting her from the hardness she felt pressing against her core. She opened her legs wider, needing to feel more, and Luke didn't disappoint. Wrapping his arms around her waist, he pulled her off the rock ledge and onto his lap, his arm pressing her firmer against him. Without hesitation, he moved one hand up into her hair and pulled her face to his, his mouth covering hers, his tongue tracing her lips until she wanted to scream. With a soft moan, she opened her mouth, his tongue gliding over hers in a way that no other ever had. The shoulders of his shirt fisted in her palms, Ami tilted her hips, bringing her breasts crashing against his chest.

"Luke," she panted when he tore his mouth away from hers and kissed her neck where her pulse throbbed in rhythm with her heart.

As he kissed his way up to her ear and then back down to the front of her throat, he released her hair, his fingers instead dipping into the neckline of her gown.

"Oh!" When he pulled back for a brief moment, her eyes widened. "Don't... don't stop."

"No," he breathed, pushing the material down to expose the tops of her breasts. She sensed his unspoken words, knew there was very little that could make him stop.

Just as Luke managed to wrestle one of Amileigh's small, but perfectly formed breasts from the top of her gown, a familiar voice rang out not too terribly far from where they were secreted away in the alcove of the cave.

"God save that man," Luke groaned, unable to resist a quick taste of the firm, petal-soft mound ovaled by his hand. Amileigh cried out when he sucked the hardened peak into his mouth, arching her back for a brief second before she collapsed against him. Five more minutes, he thought again while cradling her in his arms. Damn it to hell. If the man wasn't his great grandfather, and if he didn't know without a shadow of a doubt that he would most probably beat his ass, he'd at least go down swinging as he used his fists to alleviate some of his frustration. He wasn't sure about the beast inside, but the monster in his pants didn't know how much more it could take.

Helping Ami pull her neckline back into place, he ran a hand down her cheek, knowing even in the darkness that it was flame kissed. She stepped away and he pulled her back.

"This *thing* between us... it's going to happen," he told her staring down into her still slightly glazed eyes. When he bent to kiss her, she turned her face away.

"Not if I can help it."

When he released her, she made a show of

straightening her dress before pushing past him to begin her march down the shallow incline toward the main part of the hall. "That's just it, beautiful," he whispered from right behind her. "You can't help it. Oh," he mimicked her. "Don't stop."

Luke was momentarily startled when she wheeled around, but not enough to miss the hand that came up to slap him. Catching her by the wrist, he laughed as Kiernan materialized just a few steps away. He could just imagine the man's glare, even in the darkness. Kissing her palm, Luke dropped her hand and grabbed her shoulders, spinning her toward the man that had just saved her once again. He won't always be there, Luke wanted to say. Instead, he squeezed her derriere, earning himself an elbow to the gut before she picked up her pace and edged out in front of the two men. Kiernan gave him a raised eyebrow. Luke just chuckled and rubbed his belly. He supposed he deserved that.

No one spoke again until they'd entered the Room of Embers. Luke stopped in the entryway, stunned by the beauty of the chamber. The place had been aptly named, what with the light from yet another source above shining in to cast glowing arcs from the rock formation behind a wall of cascading water. Both Amileigh and Kiernan watched him as he moved into the room and closer to the wall of colors. He leaned over, squinting at the odd formation.

"What kind of rocks are they?" he asked, without turning toward his companions until Kiernan laughed.

"They're not rocks." He cocked a brow when Luke turned to look at him. "They're scales. Nine-hundred-year-old dragon scales, to be exact."

Luke watched Amileigh's brows raise in confusion, the perfect O of her lips making his mouth water as she whispered that she didn't know that. With a mental shake, he forced his concentration back to Kiernan. "Dragon scales? Made out of glass?"

Kiernan shrugged. "They're not glass. They just look like it." He looked at the wall, his eyes wandering over it. "This whole wall, or much of it anyway, is actually the remains of one of the mightiest of the Kedan dragons. At least he was, until he double-crossed the King of that clan, who just happened to be his brother."

"I never knew that either." Amileigh's voice softened with her astonishment.

Luke heard Kiernan chuckle. "Why would you? You always said dragons were make believe."

Letting their conversation fade, Luke's curiosity got the better of him and he inched around one side of the pool formed by the cascading water to where a section of the wall jutted out."

"It's part of a front leg, I'm suspecting."

Luke nodded. That's what he was guessing as well... provided this really was a dragon. He'd never considered their scales might be glass-like, and certainly not nearly this beautiful. The mix of yellow and amber coloring reminded him of a topaz and he thought of the yellow topaz drop pendant Mairi almost always wore. He didn't know much about it, but if memory served, it could have easily been chipped from one of these stones and wrapped in the bronzed setting with the bird at the top. He could almost see it nestled just above the valley that separated her breasts.

Frowning, he looked over his shoulder to where Amileigh studied the pool where pieces of the wall that had chipped away had managed to find their way to where she was standing. What was it Mairi had said to her? *These ruins and the beautiful castle that stood here before them have been in my family since... practically forever.* Why hadn't he thought of that before? If Mairi was a McCollum, wouldn't it stand to reason that she was a Prihom as well? He couldn't remember exactly what Kiernan had said, but if she was, then didn't it also make sense that she could have unlocked his dragon? He wouldn't have needed to cross time at all and maybe that was why he had found himself more attracted to her recently. Only she was more enamored with his brother Seth.

"Hey, Kiernan." He stood up and moved away from the wall, the splendor of it almost forgotten as he thought. "If I'm a dragon, does that mean my brothers are as well? Or, that they have the ability to become dragons, or whatever. You know what I'm asking, right?"

Kiernan was rubbing his chin as they met up. "Yes, I suppose they would, or could. Provided their paths crossed with their Prihoms."

Luke caught Amileigh out of the corner of his eye and turned as she stood from the water's edge and moved to join them.

"You were thinking of the woman, weren't you? The one that said Somerled belonged to her and her family?"

With his head cocked slightly, Luke tried to figure out her tone. Was she jealous? No, he didn't believe that was it. At least not of him and Mairi. He had to admit to himself that he was kind of disappointed. Maybe of Mairi claiming ownership to Somerled then? He smiled thinking of what she would have thought of the place before it had crumbled. With all the antiques and finery... she would have gone wild. When Amileigh cleared her throat, Luke shrugged. "I suppose. I was just wondering if Mairi's a Prihom, then why would I have needed to be sent back..."

Kiernan's laugh interrupted his comment. "Because, my young friend, provided she is one, she is clearly not *your* Prihom. Whatever we have before us, it is pretty obvious that your dragon needs to be full strength." Still laughing, he turned and placed an arm over Amileigh's shoulder. "Come on you two. We need to get back." He and Amileigh started walking toward another passageway on the far side of the cavern. "If we go this way," he called back over his shoulder, "it will spill us out not far from the back side of Somerled."

Luke looked around the room one more time before hurrying to catch up to them. Just before he did, he squatted down to retrieve one of the broken pieces from the edge of the pool only to pull his hand back. The reflection staring back at him wasn't his own, it was the breathtaking splendor of a multi-colored dragon.

Chapter 8

It wasn't until they cleared the woods, coming out at the back side of Somerled as Kiernan had said, that realization hit Luke. He stopped, turning in a complete circle on the stretch of low cut grass between the trees and the castle garden. He looked at Kiernan who mimicked the way Luke had scrunched his mouth and forehead.

"The cave runs beneath the castle."

Kiernan chuckled and nodded, even while pressing a finger to his mouth. "Not everyone knows about the caverns below, which is probably for the best. There are many ways in and many ways out, if you can see where you're going and don't get lost." He smiled and pointed to his eyes. "Another advantage of being a dragon, you can see in the dark. Maybe you've noticed that?"

Luke laughed as well. "I don't suppose those special dragon powers will help me learn how to wield a swor.... Damn!" He looked down at his hand, realizing he'd left the sword on the rock ledge where he'd laid it down to try to have another go with Ami. He held up his empty hands and Kiernan chuckled. "Guess I'm going to have to learn to hang on to it first." He and Kiernan continued their chitchat while Ami scurried the last few feet across the cobbled garden pathway, up the steps and inside the safety of the castle walls without so much as a wave or farewell.

With one last glance at his surroundings, Luke grabbed the door that his great grandfather held open and motioned for him to go inside. "Why isn't there a moat?"

"Beg pardon?" Kiernan was soothing a house in a tither over Ami's disappearance, and directing the guard to be sure Amileigh didn't leave her room without visual contact at all times.

When they were alone again, Luke went on. "I thought castles were supposed to have drawbridges and moats. This one is just out in the open." He'd never thought of it before, but there really was no protection for the huge house on the top of the hill.

Kiernan shrugged. "Moats and outer walls were used primarily as an added protection for the King or his direct descendants. The cost in time and materials wasn't deemed reasonable for anyone else."

Luke nodded. "I don't suppose the King believes in dragons either."

Kiernan stared off for a moment before answering with a low chuckle. "No, I don't suppose this one does, though there was a time the leader of the people did." Thoughts from the Dragon King rushed through his mind—visions of the mighty dragon walking in companionable silence with a man wearing a crown. He felt the sadness from the old Dragon King filling him and wondered if it would ever be possible for such a union to exist again.

"Come on, Luke. Gairlich wants us to stop by his study to fill him in on what has happened."

Luke nodded but stopped short of the door. "Can I ask you a question?"

Not sure he liked Luke's tone, Kiernan braced himself. "You may ask. I'm not at all sure I will answer."

When Luke smiled, he relaxed.

"When we were in the cave, just me and the girl... there were moments that I thought... It was almost like we could speak to each other in our minds." Luke shook his head. "Sounds crazy, doesn't it?"

Kiernan smiled and nodded. "Maybe to someone who has no idea what you're experiencing it would, but you have to remember, we share the same blood. The truth is, the minute you first touched, your transformation began. That's why you're able to communicate. Once you kissed her, the bond began to grow, and once... once you make love to her, you'll be completely transformed and have the ability to shift into dragon form."

"And only with her?"

Looking down at his toes, Kiernan thought for a minute. Obviously, it just took a Prihom and Blend, though finding those that were a perfect match was best. Normally, when a Guardian found his Prihom, there was a rush to unite and it was amiable to both parties. From the way Ami had rushed away from them, and by the questions Luke was asking, even their attraction hadn't convinced them. Stubborn kids!

"I'm afraid so." He crossed his fingers behind his back. "Once the transformation has begun, there's no going back. It's all or nothing. You either see this through to completion or live forever in a state somewhere in between." He shuffled slightly praying no errant bolt of lightning would come down and strike him for speaking his half-truth. It wasn't a lie, completely. More, it was what he wanted. He could already see the young couple together, could imagine them growing old with him and Abra, and the thought was truly appealing.

"Okay," Luke said, breaking into his thoughts. "Just so you know, I'm starting to think she's, uh... she's not half bad."

"You're a wise man, Luke." Kiernan laughed. "You come from good blood."

Shaking his head, Luke laughed as well. "You know it."

Clapping Luke on the back, Kiernan knocked on Gairlich's study door. "Yes, I do."

Amileigh couldn't get her door shut fast enough to get out of her dress. Every time it rubbed against her skin, she imagined it was him. She could feel his hands in her hair, his lips on her skin, and his body wedged between her legs.

"Get rid of this dress," she practically yelled, throwing her gown at Abigail when the young maid slipped into the room.

Abigail looked at the material mound in her arms then at her mistress. "Rid, as in..."

"Rid, Abigail. Rid! I don't care how. Bury it, burn it, cut it up into rags. Hell, you can even have it for yourself as long as I don't ever see it again. I. Don't. Care."

Ami ignored her maid's increasingly rounding eyes, knowing her behavior was completely out of character. For the second time that day, she honestly didn't care.

She walked over to the window, blew out an exasperated breath, and covered her eyes before falling into the chair. Seconds later, she felt Abigail's hand on her arm, could tell by the sounds of her breathing that the maid was kneeling at her side. She peeked out of her fingers and her eyes met the concern in the girl's upturned face.

"I'm sorry, Abigail. I just don't understand what's going on."

"T'will be all right, Milady. I do believe this is oft how one feels when love shows up."

Amileigh's hands fell to her lap and she stared at the maid as if she had grown two heads.

"Love?"

Silently, she said the word again. This had nothing to do with love. In the span of a day, she'd fallen in a pit, awakened in another time period where she'd seen her family home in ruins, and if that wasn't enough, the man from that era had somehow returned with her. Had he not, she might have been able to pass it all off as a dream. But she couldn't. Not only was he there and real, her body now ached for him. Just thinking about him sent small ripples of desire tingling through her.

And then there were the dragons. Again, she might have been able to explain the first ones away, but she'd definitely seen the one who had swooped down on her when she'd run toward the woods earlier. Just before she'd plunged into the forest, she'd turned to see him shift back into man form, her gasp barely smothered by his primeval groan as his body transformed. She knew him, the man, or recognized him at the very least. His name was Cormak Draghan, the older brother of Batair who had once tried to get her to marry him. So, they were also dragons. Amileigh nodded at the silent thought. No wonder Batair had been so set on making her his own. He needed a Prihom.

Did he still need one? Is that why Cormak was after her? Amileigh rose from the chair and went to look out of the window. She stared at the spot in the woods where she had exited with Kiernan and Luke, thankful there was nothing out of the ordinary. There would be no more man-dragon coming after her, no more shadow darkening her window or the skies above. Kiernan hadn't said so, but there was no doubt in her mind that Cormak was dead. She'd seen the remnants of blood her old friend had washed off his sword in the pool in the Room of Embers.

The pool. Brows furrowed, Amileigh slowly turned around. "Abigail," she spoke to the girl. "Fetch me my dress."

Eyes again wide with confusion, Abigail nodded and walked across the room to where she had dropped the garment when she'd gone to her mistress. She picked it up and carried it to Amileigh.

With a slight shiver, Ami ran her hand down the soft fabric before slipping her hand into the little pocket normally used to hide a lady's kerchief. She closed her palm around the jagged stone and pulled it out, holding it up to the light.

"Have you ever seen anything like this, Abigail?"

The maid shook her head while inching closer to look at the rock that glowed in the light from the window.

While she stared at it too, a faint memory flashed through Amileigh's mind. She *had* seen something similar before. Once, when she was around sixteen or so. There'd been a woman—a flower peddler. She couldn't have been much older than Amileigh was now.

If memory served, the woman had been fairly pretty—her blonde hair a lighter color than Amileigh's. She'd kept her eyes averted, even when talking directly to her and Lady McCollum. Lady Saundra had requested several of the bouquets, and that's when she'd seen it: when the woman had reached across to retrieve one bouquet in particular—a sweet mixture of roses and daisies with stems of cranberries strewn through the middle.

The stone had swung free from her gown and she'd captured it in her hand after handing Ami the bouquet. Only hers had been a deep purple with a hint of green and blue around one edge. When she'd handed her the bouquet, the woman had said something about the fragrance of love. It was only then that she'd caught her eye, winking at her before tucking the stone back inside the bodice of her dress. The memory of the woman had stayed with her for a short while, though Amileigh had mostly forgotten the whole incident, until now. What was the significance of that stone? She sucked in slightly when realization hit her.

The dragon who had been following her, standing between her and the ugly dark dragons... it had been mostly purple interspersed with patches of blue and green. *Kiernan*. Somehow that woman had managed to get hold of a piece of his scales. She was sure of it, but how, and who was she? What role did she play in all of this?

The questions plaguing Ami clouded her mind. She rushed over to her wardrobe and pulled open the double doors.

"This one, Abigail, she told her maid while reaching for one of her favorite dresses. It was a pale lilac silk with a high neck that she knew enhanced her look of innocence. The last thing she needed right now was to find herself back in the arms of the man who wanted... or needed her every bit as much as Batair.

She rolled her eyes as Abigail helped her slip the gown over her head. Her only hope against either man was to make sure she steered clear of them. That wouldn't be too difficult with Batair since he wasn't here. But the stranger... the humming in her head had already told her he was back in his room in the east wing. It may be at the far end of the hall across the stair landing, but it wasn't nearly far enough.

Clearing her throat and smoothing her hair, she picked up the dragon scale rock, slipped it in her pocket, and dismissed Abigail. She waited until after her maid left before approaching the door. Knowing a guard stood on the other side rankled her, but she knew it was for the best. If nothing else, he would see her to her destination without any handsome detours.

Back in his room, Luke paced restlessly while he waited for Kiernan to come back and get him. He wasn't sure where the other man had gone, only that he'd mentioned something about training so Luke would be ready. Ready for what? He chuckled. If it was the business with the girl, well, he had already had plenty of practice with that. He just needed Kiernan to quit interrupting him and give them time. He stopped suddenly when his heart began to race, beating hard against the inside of his chest. He put his hand over it, wondering what was happening. Then he noticed the increase in the volume of the hum.

Luke smiled and waited for the knock on his door.

As they closed the distance between her room and the stair landing, Amileigh stopped, staring down the length of the east wing.

"Are you not well, Milady?" the guard following close behind asked her when she bowed her head after pressing her fingers to her temples.

"I'm… I'm fine. I've just had a change of heart. Please," she started, turning toward him. "If you would, I'd rather go to see my mother." With a backward glance over her shoulder at the closed door toward the end of the hall, Ami started down the stairs, knowing the guard had no choice but to follow.

Lady Saundra McCollum was exactly where her daughter knew she would be. The woman spent most of her time tucked away in a well-lit corner of the library: the bound parchment pages and a grand settee her two favorite friends. Rumor had it she'd even been known to dip a quill to ink and etch out stories of her own, but if she did, Amileigh had never been privy to see any of them. She'd often wondered why, having the devotion of a man like her father, her mother found it necessary to hide in her make-believe worlds.

Ami thought of Luke. If she was married to a man like that, would she hide herself away amongst someone else's words as well? She shook her head. That was different. Gairlich McCollum loved his wife and she cared just as deeply for him.

"Ami. My darling!" Lady Saundra closed the book she was reading as her daughter approached. She sat up and patted the cushion next to her, waiting for Amileigh to situate herself before continuing. "To what do I owe the honor of this visit?" She smiled and covered Amileigh's hand with her own.

Amileigh stared at her mother as if seeing her for the first time. Her hair, with its intermingled strands of sandy brown and red, was down framing her face and making her look much younger than her nearly fifty years on this earth.

"What is it, dear? You look like you've seen a ghost." Lady McCollum glanced over her shoulder, smiling when she looked back and patted her daughter's hand in a loving gesture.

Forcing herself to smile as well, Ami shook her head. "It's nothing, Mother. I was... I just wanted to be with you for a moment."

How could Ami ever tell her mother the truth? She hadn't seen a ghost. She'd seen another woman, a much younger woman in tight fitting jeans and an unseemly shirt, in a time some six hundred years in the future. If she'd had any doubts before, there were none now. Mairi, the woman who had been with Luke at the castle ruins, had said she was a McCollum—that Somerled had been in her family for generations. No, if she'd doubted her, there was no way she could now. Mairi McCollum was the spitting image of her mother... or would have been in her mother's younger years.

The two women fell into idle chitchat until Ami could see her mother's interest was waning. With a kiss to her still soft cheek, she rose.

"I'll see you at dinner, darling," her mother called to her as she crossed the floor. "Your father tells me we're to have a most unusual guest."

Amileigh stopped. "Are we?" Her spine stiffened, she forced a smile when she turned back to see her mother's angelic countenance.

"Yes, dear. He also told me to make certain you were there." The command in Lady Saundra's voice was unmistakable.

Resisting a throaty growl, Amileigh nodded. "Of course. I wouldn't dream of missing out."

Not bothering to quiet her steps, Amileigh marched up the arched staircase and back to her room. Cahoots! They were all in on it. Even her mother who had spent well over a half of an hour talking about anything and everything that absolutely didn't matter.

Gaining entrance to her room, she leaned against the door and pulled the rock from her kerchief pocket. She should have just asked what she'd gone there to ask... what her mother knew about the flower peddler and if the rock, like the one the peddler woman wore and the one in Ami's hand, had any meaning to her. If she was a Prihom, it stood to reason her mother was one as well, didn't it? She thought back to something Kiernan had said.

Abra was right. With your parentage, you were bound to be a chosen Prihom. Chosen? What did that mean? And if her mother was Prihom, did that mean her dad was also a dragon shifter? Surely if he was, she would have seen him change or noticed... something. Then again, she had never seen Kiernan shift before either. She laughed. Was it before, or many, many, many years after? This whole turn of events was absolutely crazy.

Ami refused to change for dinner. She'd wear the lilac dress regardless of the fact that she'd already been seen in it. The idea of changing was an absurd ritual anyway. She could understand if one had been out and about, but she hadn't. At least not since she'd changed. So much silliness and fanfare, and for what? To impress a stranger?

"Are you certain, Milady? There's always the pale yellow... or even the new white."

Ami stopped her with a firm shake of her head. Both dresses showed ample amounts of skin, the yellow especially bordering on indecent in her opinion. She knew exactly what Abigail was doing. "If you don't want to find yourself in a new position scrubbing potatoes in the kitchen, I suggest you stop trying to play matchmaker."

Abigail nodded demurely and set herself to the task of finishing Ami's hair.

Satisfied with her reflection, Ami rose from the small stool in front of her dressing table and slipped into her shoes. Surely there was no way the stranger would be attracted to her now, not with her hair piled on her head and the neckline of the dress touching her throat.

At the door to her room Ami stopped and reconsidered. She thought about how it had felt when he'd raked down her body with his desire-filled eyes, how hard it had been to resist touching him when she'd gone into his room to see him sleeping. Was this really what she wanted?

With an unladylike snuff, she set her chin high and pulled open the door. Whether it was what she wanted or not, the truth was there. He didn't care for her. One slip between the sheets and he'd turn into a dragon and fly away. Ami pushed away the heaviness in her heart that descended on her with each step down the stairs. She stopped when she saw the vase of flowers on the table in the middle of the grand hall. Roses, daisies, and stems of cranberries. The hall had been filled with the scent of love.

She looked up to see Kiernan and the man enter from the parlor where they had probably stopped to have pre-dinner drinks with her father. For a brief moment she wondered if it was too late to pretend she was feeling ill and retreat to her room. Probably so, especially since he was already walking toward her.

At some point between the time they had returned from the cave and now, he'd been transformed from an oddly dressed stranger to a man almost worthy of the king's courts. Had it not been for the shadow of growth beginning to form on his face and the disheveled look of his still unruly hair, he could have easily passed for a knight. Or maybe even a prince.

Her mouth dry, she watched him approach, her cheeks flaming as he looked her up and down.

"My lady." He executed a perfect bow and offered her his arm. "You look quite lovely this evening."

With a single nod, she barely bent her knees before placing her hand on his sleeve. She recognized the garment he wore. Auley could only have hoped to ever look that good in it. Even with all his training, her brother's biceps and chest didn't strain against the material like Luke's did. She squeezed and he tapped her side with his elbow, giving her a wink when she frowned up at him.

"Ass," she mumbled into her free hand, covering it with a faked cough. Hadn't that been what Mairi had called him?

Luke chuckled and pretended to look at himself over his shoulder. "Looks pretty nice in these pants, if I might say so myself."

Rolling her eyes, Ami looked away, knowing there was no way she would be able to conceal the smile that lifted the corners of her mouth.

Ami's father had slipped by them while they were talking and was already seated at the table when they entered the dining room. Her mother, she noted, was nowhere to be seen. As usual. She'd storm in momentarily, her cheeks flushed from her scurry, and her father would smile as if the moon had just hung the most beautiful star in the sky. It was disgusting... and completely romantic, all at the same time. Ami longed for someone to look at her like that.

Just inside the door, Ami stopped Luke with a gentle tug of his sleeve when he started to walk toward the table. The seating arrangements would be altered since they had guests. Most of the time she could figure it out by their ranking, but tonight... she cast a sideways glance at Luke. Where, exactly, did this man fit in.

"Luke, Ami," Kiernan motioned them toward the other side of the table where he stood behind the chair next to her father's left. He said something and pointed to the chair beside his indicating Luke should sit there. Since Ami's brothers were filling the chairs to her father's right, save for an empty one right next to him held for his wife, she guessed she would be sitting next to Luke. Her speculation was confirmed when he pulled out the chair and waited for her to slide in before pushing it forward. Right or wrong, it was where she was sitting now.

Two places further down than her on the other side of the table, she heard Auley clear his throat and she lifted her downturned eyes to look in his direction, wishing after that she hadn't when he made several kissing motions with his mouth. Ami scrunched her nose at him and he chuckled. *Grow up*, she mouthed when he did it again.

Beneath the table, Luke's hand found hers and gave it a squeeze, pulling her attention away from her pesky twin. When his palm slipped to her thigh, her eyes went wide and she quickly looked down, thankful some matter had drawn the men at the table into a discussion that fully drew their attention away from her and Luke.

She could feel the heat through her gown, and when his fingers began to move and the material whispered against her core, Ami thought she might forget how to breathe. She kept her eyes averted, fervently studying the empty plate and silverware on the table in front of her. Without her consent, her legs opened wider and she almost gasped when his fingers pressed more firmly to her, caressing her with a gentle, circular motion. She felt herself tremble.

She didn't know what was happening, only that it was going to happen right there, in front of the men of her family. She grabbed his hand, but he held firm and she was remiss to stop him. Nothing had ever felt this good before. Help me, she thought.

I am.

The voice came through just before a flurry of yellow breezed through the door and everyone at the table began to rise.

Her mother had arrived.

Luke hadn't intended to touch Ami beneath the table, but when his hand had brushed her thigh and she'd responded, something Kiernan had said had him instantly rock hard and he had to find out.

"What about the underwear?" he'd asked when Kiernan had brought him the clothing he was to wear to dinner. Kiernan had frowned for a minute before realization had hit and he'd told him undergarments were seldom worn. Luke had decided to keep on the ones he'd shown up with, feeling a bit uncomfortable at the idea of the crown jewels swinging free beneath unfamiliar clothes.

Even before he'd touched Ami, he'd easily imagined her naked beneath the silky gown. And he'd been right to think so. There was little barrier, the heat from her body radiating into his fingers, making him press harder, wishing for more. Had she not forcefully slipped away from him when those around them started to stand up, he was sure he'd have had no trouble making her climax. Would she have screamed out? At that moment, he wouldn't have cared if she had screamed.

Dazed, he managed to tear his stare away from her and focused on the commotion across the table. The breath he sucked in when he did had him chocking on his own spit.

Staring at him as Lord Gairlich helped her into the chair next to his, an older version of Mairi covered her chest with her hand.

"My goodness, Kiernan. Perhaps you'd best give the poor man a good pat on the back."

Kiernan chuckled as Luke waved off his attempt to help. Clearing his throat, Luke followed the others back into their seats.

"Lady Saundra McCollum," Amileigh whispered from his left. "My mother."

It wasn't as if Luke had ever questioned her lineage, but if he might ever have had any doubt, that Mairi was a McCollum, he had none now. His nose crinkled as he looked down at his plate.

"Do you not care for venison?"

He glanced at Ami. "No, it's fine. I was just thinking about the future."

Luke couldn't very well tell her what he was actually thinking about. Ever since Ami's mother had sat down at the table, he'd been thinking about Mairi and wondering... since she was a McCollum, same as Amileigh, what if she was the product of one of *their* children? What if, or when rather, they finally did the big nasty, she got pregnant and had a baby... Then that baby had a baby followed by another baby... What if he'd managed to seduce Mairi and then found out she was his however many greats great granddaughter? The thought made him shudder. He was glad she'd always held her ground in her undying resolve that she would one day belong to his brother because if she hadn't, he'd have been on her in a heartbeat. The thought made him a bit sick to his stomach.

But then she would have been the one to unlock his dragon and there would be no need for him to have gone back in time, so he couldn't have been her ancestor. Right? He glanced sideways at Amileigh and felt that tingle behind the wall of his chest as he watched her pressing a piece of torn bread between her lips. She turned to him, her mouth lifting slightly at the corners and he couldn't help but return her smile. It wasn't meant to be, he thought. Maybe it *could* have happened, but it didn't, and Fate had seen fit to step in and defy time to bring him face to face with the one woman who could complete him. Mind, body, and dragon.

"So, Luke. Kiernan tells us you're related. Do you hail from around here?"

With effort, Luke turned to look at the man sitting next to Lady Saundra. He looked from the man to his mother, noting how much more he looked like her than Amileigh did. Mairi was probably the offspring of one of the men sitting across from him some six hundred years down the line. He took a deep breath feeling somewhat better about himself, though he already knew what he knew, and that was that the woman sitting next to him was made by grace and magic especially for him. All he needed to do was to convince her.

Now, what was the question? Oh, yes. He nodded slowly wondering exactly how he was supposed to answer it.

Dinner progressed with more talk than Luke would have liked. The older brothers, he learned, fought for the King and had already seen way more action on battlefields than Luke cared to think about. Someone was always trying to seize control or take another's lands, it seemed, and these men reveled in recounting the bloody escapades to see to it that didn't happen. At least as much as they could before their mother quelled them. Luke laughed thinking how Mairi would have probably egged them on, throwing in a few stories of her own.

Kiernan had fielded most of the questions aimed at him, for which Luke was extremely thankful. All he had to do was remember how Kiernan had worded things in a way that kept outright lies to a minimum. He supposed keeping secrets as long as he had that his great grandfather was a pro at it. Ami, he'd noticed, had remained mostly quiet, though every time he'd looked in her direction, she'd been fully engaged, listening and taking it all in. He'd been diligent not to touch her again, though he'd be lying if he said he hadn't wanted to. But not there.

The idea of her crying out for him to take her to the

height of passion for the first time, listening to her breathing while she arched her back and called out his name while she shattered around him... he almost groaned at the thought, knowing he didn't want to share that moment with anyone. Having her was going to be the sweetest moment of his life and just might make losing the world he lived in completely worthwhile.

Luke blinked, shocked at his own admission, though he was even more shocked when he realized everyone was staring at him. Had he missed another question or said something out loud?

"Are you finished eating?"

"What?" Luke looked at Ami, confused by her question and she nodded her head in the direction of the servants waiting nearby. "Oh. Uhm, yes. Sorry." He placed his single utensil at the top of his platter and sat back in his chair after dabbing his mouth with the cloth napkin. Almost immediately, the servants began to clear away the dishes.

Internally, Luke breathed a sigh of relief. The meal couldn't end quickly enough for him, only he should have known better. No sooner had the plates been whisked away, then they were again replaced with others. What was this? The fourth or fifth time? He heard a soft chuckle to his left when he let out a low groan and covered his stomach. Feigning a frown, he looked at Ami and she bit her lower lip in a way that had his insides boiling almost as quickly as touching her had. How could anything so sweet be so sexy?

Before he could continue that train of thought, he noticed her eyes lighting up as she looked down the table where dishes of some sort of formed custard looking dessert surrounded in glazed fruit were being set in front of her parents and Kiernan.

"Dariolles, Lady Ami. Your favorite." Kiernan leaned

forward and looked past Luke. Ami's smile told him Kiernan was correct. Luke wasn't a huge fan of custard, but he'd try it. If she liked it, it couldn't be all that bad.

The first bite when they were finally served had him considering a change in his assessment. When she laughed, he raised his brows.

"With the fruits," she whispered. "Like this." She scooped up one of the glistening strawberries, ran it through the sour tasting custard, and popped it into her mouth, licking the ends of her fingers before reaching for another one.

Luke was momentarily speechless, sure the blood rushing to his crotch was robbing his tongue of the ability to work. Breathe, he told himself as he watched her repeat the process with other fruits on her plate.

She stopped and stared at him, her cheeks reddening just before she reached forward and grabbed a small glazed cherry from his plate, scraping it through the custard and holding it out for him. Did she have any idea the innuendoes created by what she was doing? He doubted it, though instead of taking the delicate offering, he grabbed her hand and brought her fingers to his mouth, making sure his tongue grazed them before he sucked the cherry free from her grasp.

A chuckle, a cleared throat, a breathy oh, and an exasperated sigh from around them, had him letting go when she tugged away. Her cheeks flaming, she looked down, her hands clasped beneath the table in her lap. Luke looked up, and with a lopsided grin, he shrugged before grabbing another piece of fruit. Not nearly as good as the cherry, but he had to admit, it wasn't half bad, especially after he took a big gulp of the sweet Malmsey wine that had replaced the earlier drink in his goblet.

When Lady Saundra stood, followed by the other women at the table, Luke almost sighed with relief and began to push his chair back as well. Ami's hand on his shoulder stopped him and she shook her head slightly when he looked up at her. He wanted to groan when he realized the other men were still relaxed in their chairs.

"Gentlemen." The lady of the house inclined her head to the prominent males at the table. "If you will excuse us." She leaned over and kissed her husband's cheek. "Not too much port, dear," Luke heard her say before she straightened and led the other women from the room.

Luke followed Ami out with his eyes, sure he probably looked like a puppy that had just had its favorite bone taken away. When Kiernan chuckled, he looked his way, though the other man said nothing. He watched as Kiernan waved his hand, passing on the boxed cigars Gairlich was offering to him. He did the same, noticing only the oldest of the sons was offered what had to be viewed as an expensive treat, though they were all given snifters of port that nearly took his breath away when he took his first drink.

Damn, he thought. At this rate, he'd be passed out before his head even hit the pillows, or worse yet, unable to find his way down the hall once all the lights were out so that he could again sample the castle owner's sweetest treat.

Chapter 9

Luke had been right about the drink. He speculated later that its purpose was just that... to help aid the men of the house to sleep. He was terribly disappointed when he awakened the next morning only to realize they hadn't even lasted five minutes in the drawing room before Kiernan had made some excuse about him being weary from his travels and he'd dragged a bleary-eyed Luke along to their rooms. Sleep, he'd told him at the door. Luke had nodded with no intent to do so. His mind and his body wanted Amileigh. She'd been conspicuously absent from the drawing room when they got there and the first thing he intended to do was to find out why.

Sometimes the best intentions die as just that... intentions. He'd sat on the edge of the bed to remove the uncomfortable shoes that had been loaned to him, his eyes growing heavier with each blink. Closing them for a few minutes suddenly seemed like a good idea. He'd nodded. He could sleep for a bit and then go and find her. That was definitely a much better plan.

Only he'd awakened to daylight streaming in through the small window and his head felt as if a freight train had rolled through it. He groaned and rolled over, wishing he hadn't. When a knock sounded on the door, he sat up and grabbed his head, his feet just hitting the floor as Kiernan burst through the door.

"Ah, Luke! I feared the drink might have been too much for you last night when I realized the family had pulled out the better wine."

Luke glared at him with a single uncovered eye. "It

was that crap we had at the end." The thought of the port mixed with the smell of the cigar smoke made his stomach churn. "Where's the nearest bathroom?" he grumbled, uncovering both eyes when Kiernan didn't answer?

"Crap?" was all Kiernan said.

Luke shrugged, his face scrunched as if he'd smelled the stuff. "Crap," he said. "You know… badass stuff. Body excrements." He paused for a second and added bluntly. "Shit."

Kiernan just stared at him and if Luke hadn't felt so bad, he might have laughed. One thing was certain, he perplexed the man.

Turning on his heel, Kiernan marched to the door, pausing just before he left. "If it be a bath you're wanting, you'll have to wait. You'll get nothing like that until well after the noonday meal. Pointing to a screen in the corner of the room, he raised a brow. "Chamber pot and wash basin for… everything else." Just before he closed the door with a bit too much fervor, he glanced back at Luke. "I've already requested to have something sent up for your head. There are fresh clothes on the chair and Auley will escort you to the training fields once you're ready." He left without giving Luke a chance to speak.

Training fields? Luke pushed away from the side of the bed, weaving his way toward the wooden screen in the corner, praying the room would quit spinning. If that man thought he was going to make some kind of a medieval fighter out of him, he'd better think again.

Four hours later, an exhausted Luke raised his sword for the last time. At first he'd been given a wooden practice sword that felt and handled, to his surprise, much like its metal counterpart. He'd traded up from that to a diamond-shaped battle sword, and then to a longsword that made him want to sing about Excalibur. His training ended with a much shorter dagger.

When they were finished, Kiernan told him to slip the dagger into his boot. Luke had raised a brow but done so anyway. Anything to get them to let him take a break, especially since it felt like his arms were going to fall off completely if he tried to raise them again. Nothing he had ever done in his life had remotely prepared him for this. He looked at the others—Amileigh's brothers and other men that lived at or near the castle. Good Lord, they must have been ripped under the loose-fitting shirts they wore, because the majority of them had been at it since before he had arrived and they hardly looked like they were breaking a sweat. Auley sat off to the side, an older man tending to a cut that had sliced right through the cloth of his shirt. He smiled up at Luke as he and Kiernan started to walk away.

"Training bracers would have been good."

Kiernan chuckled and Luke smiled in that silly way people do when they have no idea what's being talked about.

"Saw your handiwork out there," Auley goaded him. "Thinking you might consider it as well."

When Luke stopped, a retort ready on his tongue about how he wasn't the one who got wounded, Kiernan grabbed his sleeve and nodded his head in the direction of the castle. Grumbling, Luke capitulated and went away with little more than a scathing glare at the younger man.

"He's got an attitude, Kiernan. Somebody needs to put him in his place."

Kiernan raised a brow at Luke when he spoke as they were nearing the house. "You're still sulking about that?"

He shook his head and sighed. "Truth be, he's probably right." He raised his hand when Luke started to object. "We went easy on you out there today. I put you with some of the more experienced men, those who know just how far to press. You needed training, not taken down."

Luke crossed his aching arms over his chest. *Easy!* He'd just had the hardest workout he'd ever had in his life and was being told they'd gone easy? He rolled his eyes and looked up at the sky. God help him then, because he wasn't sure he had any more to give.

As he looked down, he saw her standing with her hand pressed against the pane of glass in one of the upper floor rooms. Ami. She was watching him, or watching them rather, as they walked back across the grass. If she hadn't realized he could see her, she did when he raised his hand about face level and waved. Without returning the gesture, she backed away.

One, two, three. Luke counted the windows from the far side of the house and smiled. He'd been right. Hers was the room directly in the middle. When he and his brothers had explored the ruins, he remembered thinking the room must have belonged to a very prissy girl.

Mairi pretended to gag the first time he'd unlocked the door and shown her inside. He looked at Kiernan. His great grandfather would have known whose it was, but then Kiernan hardly ever visited the ruins of Somerled. How odd—Luke had never thought of it before. He looked around. It must have been hard for him to see it crumble since he'd walked among the halls in all their splendor, shared food and drink with the people who lived there. Still, he'd have to ask his great grandfather what had happened once he got back.

If he ever got back.

He looked up at the empty window again. It had always seemed strange to him that that part of the castle remained. Not the whole thing, of course. The outer castle wall was still there. The interior section where the back stairway and end rooms had been was gone or partly demolished, leaving those rooms and the hallway open to the elements. And with the grand main entry hall gone, he suspected having seen it now, that the upper landing had crumbled just past the huge double doors. That's where they climbed up by ladder.

Luke thought about Amileigh's room. Kiernan may not visit there anymore, but Luke suspected it was him who had installed locks on the doors of the remaining rooms, including hers. He put himself back there in modern times. Had there been any sense of deja vu?

"You coming?" Kiernan broke into his thoughts. Luke nodded, and with one last glance to the West to see that the porcelain doll had returned to her window, he followed Kiernan through the rose garden doors.

After an hour or so in Gairlich's study, Kiernan closed the book he had been looking through. Amazingly enough, there were volumes of huge books that chronicled the lives of the Kedan Blends from the time it was decided the Blends were necessary to preserve the great dragons, to the union of a couple named… Luke closed his eyes for a moment, searching for the names. Nic…Nicholas and Helaina. After many failed attempts, they were considered the first *perfect* specimens of their kind—her a purest of pure Prihom and him a perfectly bred Guardian-Dragon Blend. They'd married, of course, and Nicholas managed to transform completely, with no flaws or issues. But there was great unrest. The Dubhagan dragons wanted her, and the Kedan King's brother was in on it because he wanted power. Yada, yada, yada.

Luke pushed back, handing Kiernan the tome he had been reading. The dragon below, or what was left of it, smashed by the rock in the Room of Embers... he bet that dragon was the King's brother. He had been described on the pages as having yellows, oranges, and browns, looking as though the fire gods had lit up the sky when he flew. It must have been quite the sight to see him and his brother, the red dragon wearing the crown, in flight together. How sad that he had let his own greed get in the way and it had cost him his life. It surely must have grieved the Kedan King.

"Oooooohhhhh." Luke blew out a long breath, rubbing his forehead before rising from his chair. The only dragon he'd actually seen had not appeared to be the kind of creature who cared about anything other than its own needs. The way the one had swooped down on Amileigh, Luke could imagine it wanting nothing more than to satisfy an empty belly with a tasty morsel who had found herself in the wrong place at the wrong time. That's what he remembered of dragon folklore... they ate people.

And breathed fire. Good grief! Luke crinkled his nose. Did that mean he would breathe fire? He sure hoped not. Honestly, that sounded a bit disturbing to say the least.

He realized Kiernan had been watching him in his reverie. With a lopsided smile, he shoulder bumped his great grandfather.

"What's a guy gotta do to get some food around here?" After the workout they'd had, he was about ready to storm the kitchens if someone didn't offer him food soon. And no wine. He didn't care if he ever drank again. Double emphasis on *ever*!

Disappointment edged in when Amileigh didn't join them for the midday meal. He overheard an excuse being made to her father about her being *femininely predisposed*. He wasn't sure what that meant, but it made both Kiernan and Gairlich frown.

At dinner, which came after a bit more cave exploration, a strange but warm bath, and a short rest, they were told Amileigh's head was hurting too much for her to join them. Her head his ass, Luke thought. He closed his eyes, stilling his thoughts.

You can't hide from me forever, he thought. The returning silence made him doubt it had gotten to where he'd intended.

Finally, after several moments, words not his own zinged into his head. *Four days.*

Luke scrunched his face. *What does that mean?*

He was sure he could hear her laughter. *Ask Kiernan the date.*

The date? Had they set a wedding date or something.

"Hey, Kiernan," Luke interrupted the conversation. "Is there something I need to know about the date?"

"The date?" Lady Saundra said, echoing the words of one of her sons. Gairlich's lips thinned, and Kiernan pushed two fingers against his forehead as he looked sideways at Luke.

"Can't see anything that could be considered special about a Wednesday," Auley piped in, all eyes turning to him.

"Wednesday? What are you talking about?" Luke squinted at the younger man who somehow managed to continuously annoy the crap out of him.

"I think you're just overly tired, my friend."

Luke shrugged away the hand Kiernan tried to place on his arm, alarm rising inside him at the placating tone.

"She says four days." He glared at the younger version of the man he knew. "What's going to happen, Kiernan? I think I have a right to know."

The silence at the table made the scraping of the legs of Kiernan's chair sound even louder than it should have. When he stood, Luke followed suite.

"Forgive us, my lord." Kiernan made a show of a slight bow toward Gairlich, not looking at anyone else, including Luke, as he stormed out of the room.

Luke tried to mimic the bow then waved a hand in front of himself and skirted out. To hell with it all, he thought. This was his life these people were playing with.

"What's happening in four days, Kiernan?" he practically yelled. At least he'd held his cool until they'd passed the grand hall staircase and were on their way down the hall that held Gairlich's study. At this time of night it was the most secluded. "Damn it!" He grabbed Kiernan's arm, stopping him and wheeling him around.

Squared off, the two men stared at each other until Kiernan stepped back. Bowing his dark head, he brought his hands up, blowing against his palms.

"It wasn't only you who went back in time," he said in a low, quiet tone.

Luke squinted. His lips puckered as he tried to make sense of what Kiernan had said.

Finally, the younger man looked up at him. "It was Sunday, the day you were at the ruins?"

Luke nodded. "But I don't see…"

"Ami said it was Sunday as well. She said we'd gone

out for a ride that afternoon, only..." Kiernan looked away then back before continuing. "Luke, the ride was supposed to happen this coming Sunday."

Sucking in a quick, deep breath, Luke stepped back. He stared at Kiernan as if he'd grown a second head. "Holy crap."

Kiernan stared at him. "Crap. Excrement." He shook his head. "I don't think that can be holy."

Had the situation not been so monumental, Luke might have laughed, choosing instead to ignore it. "So, what does all this mean?"

Shrugging, Kiernan looked over his shoulder. "I have no idea."

Following his gaze, Luke turned around to see Gairlich's large, commanding body zeroing in on them.

"Gentlemen. I will tell you what you already know and that is these walls have ears." He looked at the crack in the wall that would have easily allowed in a man turned sideways. "Perhaps we should continue this in my study."

Both men turned to follow him and Luke smiled. "Kiernan? Wouldn't the books hold the answers?"

Kiernan frowned. "The books?" After a second, his brows shot up. "Ah, the tomes."

Gairlich barely managed to unlock the door before they rushed in to the cabinet where he kept them, waiting impatiently until he unlocked that as well. Pulling each book out and turning to the end, the men went through all twelve of the large volumes rather quickly. Several of them Luke had to hand to Kiernan because he couldn't understand the language of that time. Even with that, they made quick work of the task, both staring in disbelief when they scanned for a date on the last book.

"We must have missed it," Luke said, reaching for one

of the discarded volumes.

Kiernan shook his head. "It's not here." His shoulders slumping, he sunk down in Gairlich's desk chair.

Counting, Gairlich looked puzzled. "It was. There were thirteen yesterday. Now there are only twelve."

"Twelve what, dear?"

The three men turned to see Lady Saundra standing at the door. She looked from them to the books strewn about. "Oh, the old tomes." She walked over and ran her hand down the front of the cover of one on the edge of the desk. "Are you looking for the last one?" When Kiernan nodded, she smiled. "I'm sorry. I have it."

"You! Why?"

Dressed in a modest dusty rose colored gown, the vision floated across the room to where her husband stood. "Please, dear, don't be mad. I just wanted to read it." She caressed his cheek. "I've read them all through the years." She looked at Luke. "I remembered something after we met yesterday. A name... Loukas. You were foretold centuries ago." She walked over to him. "You're going to take my daughter away, aren't you?"

Luke blinked down at her. Was he? "We need the book."

The three men followed Lady Saundra to her room which was just a few doors down from Ami's. Luke and Kiernan stood respectably in the hallway until her words alerted them that the book was not there.

"I don't understand." She stood with her hands pressing her cheeks. "It was here earlier."

"Perhaps it's in the library, dear. Don't you usually read in there?"

She was already shaking her head when she turned to

her husband. "I specifically brought it here."

When Luke let out a string of expletives under his breath, all eyes turned on him. "Sorry, I just…"

"It's disappointing, I know. I'd wanted to finish, had thought I'd be able to read after dinner." Lady Saundra shrugged. "It will turn up. I'm sure of it. Or maybe it's better that we don't know beforehand."

The grumbled responses from the men showed all three disagreed. Gairlich mumbled something about he and his wife discussing how she'd even managed to gain access to his study, let alone the sacred volume. She'd responded with her own mumbled words about magic.

As they were filing out of the room, the shaking of the earth below had them all pressing against the wall. It didn't last long, just enough to unnerve them. Luke thought for a minute. Wasn't it Wednesday when he and Will had first found the door?

As a group, they looked up when Amileigh's door opened. Luke sighed when her wide, lilac eyes locked with his. She looked away quickly, though it didn't matter. Lady Saundra was already rushing to her, blocking his view.

"It's okay, love. Just a tremor. Nothing to be concerned about."

Luke watched mother soothing daughter and his heart filled. Would that someday be Amileigh with his child? He tried to pull up an image of it, but the only thing he saw was the guard moving to block her door as Lady Saundra ushered her daughter back inside, telling her she'd stay with her if she liked. If he was forced to stay away from her, he wasn't sure how he would ever unlock his dragon, let alone how they were to produce a child.

Exasperated, he shrugged away when Kiernan tapped

his arm to let him know they were going back downstairs. Luke mumbled some excuse and went to his room instead. Where the hell was that book, and what else lay in the belly of this castle behind that door the guard with the Conan build had gone through when he was in the holding cell? Somewhere within these walls, or beneath them, Luke felt sure he would find the answer to why he was there.

You don't need to see to know.

Luke lay quietly in the middle of his bed. That voice had sounded from deep within. It was his dragon, not Amileigh.

Amileigh.

Thoughts of lilac eyes and petite breasts filled his mind as he drifted to sleep. And touching her without barriers.

Chapter 10

Luke woke up the next morning surprised his sheets weren't due for a changing. He and Amileigh had done some amazing things in his dreams. Groaning, he turned over. He was sore beyond belief from his training, but he still smiled. Soon, he thought, throwing back the covers. He'd already decided he was through leaving anything else to Fate.

His strength renewed by his conviction, Luke put his all into his four hours of training that morning and even Auley was smiling for real by the time they were finished. He grabbed Luke by the forearm just before he and Kiernan left the field. Leaning in, he mumbled something about Luke having a good day then added ever so quietly, "The guard leaves her room for an hour each day, just after the noonday meal so that he may relieve and replenish himself."

Luke squinted, staring into the darker version of Ami's eyes. Why was Auley telling him this?

"I am his replacement during that time," he continued in the low whisper. "It's a boring job, so today I may have to slip to my room for a moment or two just after I take over the shift." His blonde eyebrow lifted just before he glanced past him. Straightening up, Auley clapped Luke on the back, jesting about beginner's luck.

Still perplexed, Luke laughed anyway, playing along as he turned to see Kiernan walking back toward him from where he'd moved away to talk to someone else. He glanced back over his shoulder as they walked away and Auley nodded at him.

Why, he thought, would her twin want to help him get in with his sister?

As they cleared the woods and began the trek across the lawn, Luke looked up, his heart jumping when he again saw her at the window. Below the tie that held up his pants, his cock jumped too and Luke decided the why didn't matter. If she was going to refuse to see him, he'd just have to go to her. Wasn't that what he'd said this morning? The ball was in his court. It was time for him to take the shot.

"Three points," he mumbled as they stepped foot inside the castle door.

Amileigh hadn't joined them for the midday meal again. Luke would have been surprised if she had. He considered ribbing her over it via their strange mind speak, but was concerned he'd somehow give away his plans.

The meal had been quite jovial, though Luke knew it might have just been him. Ever since he and Kiernan had returned after his little talk with Auley, he'd been unable to keep a smile off his face and an extra spring out of his step. He'd joined in the laughter and the revelry as much as he could for someone who had none of the same experiences. Shortly after the trenchers had been cleared, Auley rose, catching Luke's eye as he did. The younger man gave a curt nod and Luke returned it before quickly looking away, hopeful no one had caught the slight action. Now all he had to do was find a way to break away from Kiernan. Even that little concern couldn't dampen his spirits.

When they left the dining room a few minutes later, he raised a brow at Kiernan's sideways glance.

"That song? I don't know it?" Kiernan told him.

Luke frowned, then shrugged. "Didn't even realize I was humming one." He chuckled.

"Hmm. Anything you need to tell me about?" Kiernan crossed his arms over his chest, stopping so Luke had to as well.

Damn. Luke knew he'd better rein it in. Kiernan had already told him that he and Gairlich had petitioned the church for a rushed marriage and for him to not try to *persuade* Amileigh into anything until they heard back. Luke hadn't answered, so technically he wasn't breaking his word by what he was about to do.

"No, sir," he answered.

Now it was Kiernan's turn to frown. "Sir?"

Luke shrugged. "Just a show of respect in my day."

"Ah. Well, I wanted to tell you that Gairlich has been summoned to the monastery and I believe it would be a good idea if I escorted him."

Nodding slowly, Luke covered his mouth with his hand, hoping it looked as though he was thinking and not covering a chuckle, which he was. Inside he was pumping his fist and jumping in the air. This was going all too well.

Kiernan went on to tell Luke that Auley would be available to him once the lad, as Kiernan called him, had completed his post meal duties. Kiernan didn't elaborate on what Auley had been commissioned to do, but that didn't matter. Luke already knew exactly what *the lad* would be doing during his duty time today. The men parted company with Luke claiming he thought he might spend some time resting in his room.

Luke did go to his room, but only long enough to freshen up. He didn't really want to share space with the prim, little blonde smelling like the men on the training field or with pottage in his teeth. If he'd been back home, a hot shower and a toothbrush would have done the trick. Here, he had to settle for a pitcher of tepid water, some strange but appealing smelling herbs, and a cloth with something akin to peppermint oil rubbed across his teeth. At least there was some form of hygiene. The thought of Amileigh's cranberry rose scent had him groaning, his cock pressing at the hand sewn seam of his borrowed pants.

"Not yet, boy," he mumbled to it. "You need to let me use the head on my shoulders to get us there."

Amileigh's eyes pivoted to her door, and she quickly pushed herself to a standing position next to the small writing desk in the corner. Her hand on her chest, she stared, wide-eyed at the man now leaning against the inside of her closed door.

"Wha... what are you doing? You can't just barge in here! I can't be alone with a man in my chambers. You'll ruin me. You'll..." Amileigh had found her voice as she skirted around her bed and headed toward the most irritating man she had ever encountered in her entire life. All twenty-three years of it.

She squinted, her head cocked slightly as she neared, making sure to stay just beyond an arm's length away, his lack of words unnerving her. He was simply watching her, leaning against the plank, his palms against the wood.

"Are you not well? What has happened? Where's Kiernan?" Her voice rose with each question. Unfortunately, so did her rate of breaths when he still did not answer.

After a few more seconds, he stepped forward. Amileigh stepped back.

"What are you doing?" she whispered when he reached out and, taking hold of her upper arms, pulling her closer, though leaving some distance between them. "Tell me." Her demand was weak.

Her eyes locked with his, she frowned, unsure of what she saw in their depths. He looked almost pained causing her heart to clench. She watched, mesmerized, as he licked his lips.

"I need," he said at last, his voice soft as he gently pulled her closer to him, one hand slipping down around her waist, the other snaking up to the back of her neck beneath her long hair. "I need to sleep with you," he whispered, practically against her slightly parted lips.

"You *what*?" She pulled away, ignoring the surprised raising of his brows. "You have your own room in the guest wing," she scoffed. "Go and sleep there."

Pushing him away, Ami began to retreat further into the room, only to be stopped by his hand on her arm. She looked at his hand and then at him, her lilac eyes filled with annoyance, especially when Luke chuckled.

"You don't understand. I *need* to *sleep* with *you*." He stared at her as if his inflections should impart complete understanding.

She shook her head. "Are you mad? I do not wish to sleep, especially with you." Having jerked away again, she glared at him with her hands on her hips. "Besides, you shouldn't even be in here. Where's my guard..."

Luke grabbed her again when she moved toward the door, turning her to face him. "Look. I need you. I mean, I really, really *need* you. I've tried everything, baby. Believe me, I've tried, but there's just no release. My damn dick's so hard... it's like all the effects of Viagra without the little pills. Geez!" He released her and ran his hands through his hair. "All the damn commercials say to go to the doctor if general stays at salute for more than four hours. Whatever this is..." He waved his hand between them. "It's not going away. Kiernan says you're the only one who can unlock my dragon, and I'm guessing this damned hum isn't going anywhere either until we do the big dance." He pulled her close again, his gaze shifting between her eyes and her lips.

"Let go of me." Her demand was weak.

"I can't," he whispered. "Not now. Not ever."

When his mouth descended on hers, Amileigh felt her knees go weak. Good Lord, this couldn't happen. The *this* he was talking about wasn't just kissing her, or even fondling her breast as he had in the cave. The thought had sparks exploding inside her every bit as much as his tongue sliding between her lips, and the thought of his hand on her at dinner... those feelings were why she had been doing her best to stay away from him.

"Ami," he moaned against her mouth. "Sweet Ami. You," he said breathlessly. "You were meant for me."

"Meant," she whimpered back. Yes. She'd crossed time, and so had he, just to be together. When his hand slid down her back to cup her rear and press her against him, Ami moaned at the ridge she felt against her lower belly. Without ever having been told, she knew exactly what it was and what it meant, especially when he began to move against her and she felt her very core reaching out, yearning for him.

When he turned them and began moving toward the bed, she let him for the first few steps. It would have been so easy for her to have fallen back on the coverlet, to have let him lift her skirts and plunge deep inside, satisfying them all... woman, beast, and man.

But she couldn't.

"No," she whispered weakly, then more forcefully when she pulled out of the kiss. Staring up at him, certain the smoldering desire in his eyes was reflected in her own, she swallowed the knot in her throat. "If you care about me at all," she croaked out, "you'll not do this. Because if you do, know that it is completely against my will."

Reality soaked Luke like a bucket of ice water and he stopped immediately. Against her will, his ass. She wanted him. He knew it. In fact, he knew she wanted him every bit as much as he wanted her, and that if he could get his hand beneath her skirt, he'd find her wet and ready. But damn if he was going to take a woman who claimed she didn't want it. Even if he knew she was lying.

Moving his hands to her upper arms, he put her away from him. Her lovely face crinkled in confusion. Why, he thought, staring at her? Had she honestly thought he would ignore her comment? And if he had, what then? Would she have seen him confined to the dungeon again?

Luke shook his head and turned away, walking to the door without saying a word. Before turning the knob, he looked back to where she still stood watching him. His ethereal vision. Perhaps Kiernan would return with good news from the monastery. Otherwise, he might never have the opportunity to truly make her his own.

Quietly, he opened the door, closing it softly when he was on the other side. *If you change your mind, you know where to find me*, he thought as he walked down the hall to his own room. Nothing came back to him. Perhaps she hadn't heard. Or perhaps she had simply decided to ignore him. Either way, Luke slipped into his room wishing like mad for the ability to take a cold shower.

Chapter 11

Luke chose to stay in his room during dinner that night. He'd heard Kiernan and Gairlich had not yet returned and, truthfully, the idea of small talk with the rest of them was more than he could bear. He'd eaten what they'd sent up and settled in for an early bedtime. Hopefully Kiernan and Gairlich had had a better day and would return with news tomorrow. Though, if she didn't want him, could Luke bring himself to marry her knowing that? He shrugged against his pillow. He needed her to unlock his dragon. They still didn't know what was going to happen when Sunday rolled back around, but Luke felt certain he needed to be ready, and that included allowing the beast his freedom.

She does want you, the voice inside rang out.

Luke thought of the fire in her eyes. Physically, she did. But he wanted her to want him in every way. He was willing to give her every part of him… his body, his dragon, and his heart. She was his key, his Prihom. Was it too much to ask for her heart as well?

Luke fell asleep with way too many thoughts running through his head, but only one that mattered. Luke Tavish was afraid he had finally fallen in love.

Amileigh paced around her room not too unlike the caged animal she had become. When Luke had left her earlier she had collapsed on her bed, sobbing until her tears would come no more. The door closing behind him felt like a weight slamming against her heart and she didn't understand why. What he was asking of her wasn't right. Ladies went to their marriage bed with their virtue intact, and gentlemen understood that, taking mistresses when necessary, to assure such indiscretions did not arise.

But this was different. Luke wasn't of her world and there was no guarantee he would remain there. If she awakened the next morning to find him gone, what then? Could she bear the thought of going through her entire life not having known the love of the one man she knew had been created just for her?

With her heart slamming against her chest, Amileigh set into motion the plan that had begun to hatch in her head. As she pinned the scrawled note to the pile of clothing she had placed beneath the covering of her bed, she heard the same words she had heard before she'd climbed from the pit. She'd been uncertain then as well.

Opening her door just a crack, Amileigh looked for the guard, motioning him forward when he stood from the large chair positioned next to the table across from her room. She'd implored him to get her maid, praying Abigail would read the note and understand, doing all that she asked. The guard hadn't wanted to leave, but she'd finally convinced him, stating she wasn't well and needed her servant's ministrations. Reluctantly, he'd gone off, and Ami had counted to a patient ten.

Don't think. Act.

Amileigh slipped out of her room, knowing there would never be another man for her. Not now. Not ever.

When Luke felt the softness of a warm body sliding up next to him, he was certain he was dreaming. Having

Amileigh climb into his bed had been a recurring fantasy pretty much since he'd been at Somerled. But when cold hands touched his skin, he opened his eyes to see the most beautiful sight he'd ever seen—Ami staring back at him, her dilated eyes aglow in the moonlight.

"Good Lord, what…"

"Shhh." She pressed her fingers against his lips "Don't speak," she whispered, "Just make love to me."

Dear God, Luke suddenly couldn't breathe. Was this for real? He'd already determined that, and yet… he wrapped his arms around her naked body, rolling her to her back and crushing his lips to hers in fear she would evaporate.

"You changed your mind," he told her, pulling back, trying to rein himself in so he could savor every moment.

Ami shook her head. "I didn't change my mind, Luke." He frowned and she smiled. "I wanted you from the moment I first laid eyes on you… six hundred years from now."

"And four days," he added, unable to suppress his grin.

"Technically," she added with a chuckle, using the word she'd heard him use, "Three days now. It's well past midnight."

"Past midnight?" When she nodded, he continued. "Well, then we'd better get busy here." He pushed up so that he could look down the length of her beneath him. "You're beautiful," he told her.

"And you have already begun to see in the dark." They laughed softly before the seriousness of the moment took hold.

"Are you sure?" he asked, staring into her eyes, pleading with her to say yes.

Ami nodded. "More certain than I've ever been…

oooh!" Her affirmation dissolved into a moan of pleasure as Luke moved with dragon swiftness and she found his head positioned between her legs, his mouth firmly over her wet, swollen bud. "Luke." Her hands in his hair, knees falling wide, she squirmed beneath him. He hadn't meant to start there, but after days and nights, imagining the sounds she would make, he needed to hear it, and fast. As he circled the folds with his tongue that he knew would make her scream, he savored her taste—sweet mountain cranberries, with just a hint of rose scent.

Amileigh wasn't sure what she'd been expecting, but this had not been it. Not that she was complaining. Her head and her world were spinning way too fast for that. When Luke had first descended on her, she'd had concerns. Her knowledge of relations between men and women were limited to what she'd seen in the animal world, and of course the statues in the king's forbidden garden. That day in the cave when he'd suckled her breast... she'd thought she would explode, but even that did not compare to this. The more he licked and taunted her with his mouth, the higher she felt. Her body thrust itself toward him of its own will, her back arching, hips bucking. When he slid a finger inside her, she thought she might scream, or perhaps she did. She'd felt him chuckle and add another one, stroking her insides with a rhythm that matched her thrusting dance.

"Luke," she called out, her hands grabbing for the mattress beneath her. He had his free hand beneath her hips, pulling her back to him every time she tried to squirm away. It wasn't that she wanted away, it just... God, she had never felt anything so intense.

With every thrust and every lick, the need inside her rose until she was certain she could take no more. And then something glorious happened. Luke's face was again even with hers and she could feel him pressing into her. She pressed back and he slid deeper and deeper still. Ami moaned and he growled, gently nipping her lower lip. Their eyes locked, it was obvious he was remiss to miss what was happening.

"Luke," she whispered as he began to move inside her.

"Yes. Oh, Amileigh." He was almost as breathless as she was. "Look at me, baby. I want to see your eyes when you shatter. Keep climbing, love. Climb. That's it."

Coaxing her with his words and his body, Ami clung to him, her nails raking down his back, digging into the hard muscles as she let them slide lower. Nothing had ever felt so good, so right. She slipped one hand over his hip, pressing it between them, wanting to feel their union. Luke let her, slowing down only for a second until her fingers touched his engorged shaft plunging in and out of her. Ami had never sexually touched a man's naked body. She'd never seen one, actually... except on one of the statues in the forbidden garden, and that only briefly before her brothers had pulled her away saying it was something she should not be looking at. She would look at Luke, once they were finished because she wanted to see, wanted to know of this thing that he had used to make her feel this way. Surely it must be beautiful, because their union was, and after she looked, she would trace her tongue over every line of his ink.

When she pulled her hand away, Luke grabbed it, bringing it to his mouth where he kissed her fingers, licking along their undersides much as he had with the custard from the Dariolles at dinner. Just as it did then, it took her breath away and her insides clinched, tightening around him. Her breath coming in quick gasps, she wrapped her legs around his waist just as Luke reached for one of the hardened peaks of her tight breasts. Ami screamed his name as he rolled it between his thumb and finger, her hips bucking violently against his as wave after wave of earth-shattering pleasure exploded at the depth of her core and she watched all control leave him, just before the hot liquid, his very essence, poured into her. Luke collapsed on top of her— both of them breathing hard, her body still tingling, her sex still pulsating around him. They were one now in every way and he'd been right. She was his key. When his seed had begun to flow into her, she'd stared into his eyes, and in that moment, she had seen his dragon.

They made love several more times throughout the night, exploring and learning one another as new lovers do. After the last time, Ami nuzzled his chin and kissed him soundly before sitting up. "I have to get back to my room before the household begins to wake," she told him, looking at the window where the sky was maybe only a hint lighter than it had been in the hours before. She laughed when he groaned. "Abigail can't lure the guard away forever. I can guarantee he will return well before the sun begins to rise."

Luke nodded even though he still didn't like the idea of her leaving. So, she'd enlisted the help of her maid to get her to him. Inside, he'd chuckled. He supposed he should have wondered, but hadn't. With Ami's body next to his there was no way he'd been able to think about anything else. But she was right. There was no need for anyone else to know how the two of them had spent their night. At least not yet.

He watched her slide from the bedside and reach for the gown she'd discarded—the one he'd not even seen. She smiled as she stepped into it, though he thought he saw a spec of sadness in her eyes.

"You're free now... you and your dragon. You'll be able to change now and do whatever it is you've been called to do, whether in my world or yours."

He understood her fears because he had them too. There was no certainty in any of this, and yet she'd given herself to him freely, providing him with such special gifts. He slipped from the sheets to stand beside her.

"You are my key, my Prihom, Ami. You unlocked the world for me." He kissed her on her shoulder before pulling the gown up to cover the spot. "In exchange, my heart, my body, my dragon will always belong to you... no matter how much time separates us."

She turned her face up and he kissed her, wishing he could take her back to bed. A few more minutes or a lifetime... he would settle for either, just to have her near.

"I have to go," she whispered.

Luke nodded, placing his forehead against hers. When Kiernan and her father returned, perhaps they'd marry immediately and there'd be no more sneaking about. He'd never really relished the thought of being able to hold someone in his arms as often as he liked before, but he did with her.

Ami smiled. "Perhaps the special license will be granted. I heard Father and Kiernan had ridden to the monastery to find out."

Luke almost choked on his next breath. "You knew?" She nodded and he found himself blinking back the strange moisture that had sprung to the corners of his eyes. She had known they could be married soon and still she had come to him. After one more encompassing kiss that told her how much he loved her, he took her hand and led her down the hall.

"I'll be down for dinner," she told him as she slipped into her room. "My mother has given me no choice."

"Until then, my Lady." Luke kissed her hand and stepped back, bowing when she curtsied.

"Until then, my Lord." She blew him a kiss and shut the door.

Whistling softly, Luke began the lonely trek back to his own room, stopping abruptly after just a few steps. The floor swayed and he reached for the wall. It was strangely cold beneath his palm, an even cooler breeze suddenly gusting from out of nowhere as the world around him dissolved into rippling waves. He looked down to see the lush tapestry rugs melt into rotting carpet.

"What the hell?"

In the distance, he could see the lanterns that hung every few feet along the hall and watched them turn into stars, one falling to the floor before him near the big double doors. He squinted. It wasn't a lantern or a star, but an industrial flashlight. And there was a person sitting beside it.

"Will?"

His younger brother turned his face toward him, though Luke felt more like he was looking through him than at him. Will let the bottle drop away from his mouth and his lips curved up in a drunken grin while he pushed himself up onto unsteady feet.

"Get away from the edge, Will." Luke reached for him, but he couldn't move. "Will!" he called again when his brother stumbled, barely managing to right himself. Will just laughed, sliding back down to his rear and scooting to where his legs dangled over the edge near the ladder.

"Oh, God." Luke held his breath, frustration at his

inability to move making him swear. "I told you not to climb up here to drink. You stupid kid, you're going to kill yourself climbing down one of these days."

"I know, I know, Brother." Will laughed again and swung his foot toward the ladder. "If you were here, I know zezactly what you would tell me. To get my ass down and stay down." He reached for the ladder, nearly stopping Luke's heart when he faltered before finally managing to grab hold.

"Come on, Kid," he whispered, closing his eyes as Will's head disappeared below the severed floor. He winced when, seconds later, a commotion indicated a fall.

"I'm okay," his brother's voice floated up and Luke's breath whooshed out just before the earth let out another rumble. Swaying with the tremor, he stepped forward.

"No!" he screamed as the gap in the structure before him began to take form. "Will!" Stumbling, he scrambled down the stairs that were only partially there, rounding the corner, the walls solidifying just as he saw Will staggering in a direction that could only mean one thing. He knew where Will was going. To the metal door, and the dungeon below.

Luke blinked several times, scrunching his eyes closed and then opening them wide, trying to rid his head of the vision. What the hell was happening? Had he actually seen his brother in the future or was the whole scene just a trick his mind was playing on him? Reality was becoming a blur.

On heavy limbs, Luke climbed back up the stairs, pausing on the landing to stare down the hall of the family wing. The guard sitting in the chair across from Amileigh's door, just as he was supposed to, looked in Luke's direction, but said nothing. Another servant was beginning to turn up the oil lamps on the wall, relighting the ones that had been extinguished for the night. All seemed right in their world.

Luke sighed and turned toward the guest wing where he wouldn't even bother to remove his clothing before he collapsed onto the bed. He breathed deep, reaching for the sheet and pulling it to his face. It smelled of her... of them. He'd just had the most wonderful night—more magical than he could have ever imagined, and yet his heart was weighted down with concerns about his brother. He fell asleep and dreamed of Will.

Heavy pounding had Luke on his feet before his eyes could even open. Sonofa... he staggered to the door after realizing where the sound was coming from. With a glare that could have cut down the hardest of men, he pulled open the door to come face to face with Kiernan.

The older man glared back for a second before pushing past Luke, stalking around the room as if he was looking for something. Luke felt his heart pounding when Kiernan stopped, crossed his arms over his chest, and stared, lifting one brow. It was a look Luke had seen often from his great grandfather during his youth... one that always indicated displeasure.

"Tis nearly noon. Why are you still in bed?"

Luke blinked a couple of times in rapid succession before averting his eyes. Did Kiernan suspect what had happened between him and Amileigh, or was he simply annoyed that Luke had missed his training? He looked everywhere but at his great grandfather, not wanting to give anything away.

"I... uh..." He fished for something, anything to say. "I saw my brother," he finally blurted out, looking up.

"Your... brother?"

Luke nodded, rushing on to tell Kiernan about seeing his brother. He was careful with what he said, leaving out minor details like which side of the stairs he'd been on or why he was out of his room at that time.

Kiernan rubbed his chin as he listened, nodding occasionally. "And you actually saw him go to the door that leads down to the dungeon?"

Squinting, his brows down, Luke started to nod, then stopped. He hadn't seen him at the door, not exactly. But he knew without a doubt that is where Will was headed. "Well, he had rounded the corner and was making his way down that hall when everything changed back to the present. Or, to now… which is really the past, but present." He shrugged. "That's when I lost him."

Kiernan straightened his stance and slowly nodded. "I see." He looked at Luke for a second before again surveying the room, stopping to stare at the unmade bed. "Luke. Tell me what happened."

Luke swallowed hard. "I… already did."

Kiernan's piercing blue eyes swung back to him and he shook his head. He spoke in a low, deep voice, filled with command. "As far as I'm concerned, you and the girl are as good as married. You will do right by her, do you understand?" Not waiting for the nod that Luke gave, he continued. "Now get ready. We must ride out so that you may learn to release your dragon."

Luke didn't move for a few minutes even after Kiernan brushed past him and left the room. Just like in his own time, Kiernan seemed to know everything without really knowing. Maybe it was his dragon sense. Luke wondered if he would develop it, kind of like the night vision. He thought of the vision that had been in his bed the night before and felt a stirring in his pants. He groaned. As much as he'd like to entertain those thoughts, now really wasn't the time for it. When Kiernan had mentioned releasing his dragon, Luke had instantly felt the straining, a burst of excitement rippling through him.

Wait, he thought turning toward the screen so he could wash up. *Ride out?* "Oh brother!" He hadn't been on a horse since he was maybe thirteen. This might well be a day of great humility.

Chapter 12

Riding seemed to come naturally to Luke, much to his surprise. At least it did once he managed to get himself up in the saddle. If the damned horse hadn't started moving before he could hoist himself up, it would have made a huge difference. Maybe if he hadn't been distracted when he looked up at a certain window it would have gone better, but he did eventually get atop the large beast and found he enjoyed the feeling, especially as they galloped across the countryside. He wasn't sure where Kiernan was taking him, though he figured it had to be far enough away so that no one would see them when they changed or took to the skies. Another surge of excitement shot through him and he felt his dragon straining inside.

Ami couldn't help but laugh as she watched Luke attempt to get on his horse. She wasn't sure how people got around in his time, but if she had to make a wager, she'd guess it wasn't of an equine nature.

His time. She smiled thinking how she'd tried to deny her feelings for the man from the future, only to find her attraction to him was beyond her control. At least it seemed that way. When he'd come to her room, she'd been a whisper away from submitting. Only he'd stopped abruptly, leaving her feeling more alone than she'd ever felt. Even more than when she was in the pit. She shivered and pushed away the thoughts of her captivity. She didn't want to think about that. Just Luke, and how as one day had slipped into the next, she'd succumbed to the desire that had been building in her since he'd left her room, admitting to herself that the more she'd tried to smother the flames, the bigger they'd grown until they'd threatened to consume her. In her mind, visions of them together filled her head. Skin on skin, mouths, tongues, and... already her breath was growing shallow just thinking about him touching her.

Wanton. Her thoughts were wanton, and yet she refused to feel bad. Nothing could have convinced her more than the night they had just shared that Luke was the man Fate had intended for her. How they had been separated by six hundred years was anyone's guess. It really didn't matter. All had been made right, and if she was correct, her father's and Kiernan's return meant the special license had been granted. In just a few days, they would be married before men.

As the sun when behind a cloud, she winced and stepped away from the window. It had been a cloud, had it not? She shook her head and peeked out again, looking out at the sun shining down over the trees. She rubbed her hands up and down her arms, wishing for Luke's arms to be around her again.

Kiernan was mostly quiet while they rode, leaving Luke's mind free to jump from subject to subject. Steering his mind away from thoughts of Ami, and not wanting to overly excite the already exuberant beast inside, he tried to remember what had happened back home leading up to him and Mairi visiting the Somerled ruins on Sunday. When Will hadn't returned to the manor on Friday morning, no one had thought anything of it, but by nightfall and not hearing from him, they had begun to worry.

He may have been a grown man, but he'd always be the kid brother. With Kiernan away, Abra had taken charge, asking Luke and Mairi to take her to the old ruins. She felt certain that's where the youngest Tavish would be. In the dark, they'd looked around, calling as they went, and finding nothing. Now, knowing what he did, Luke couldn't help but to be more worried, not that there was anything he could do about it from there.

When Saturday rolled around in his own time, he and Mairi had gone back to the ruins to not only investigate more into Will's potential whereabouts, but because there had been more tremors in the night and Kiernan always wanted them to check things out when that happened. Whether he was away or not, Kiernan's will seemed to get things done. Luke smiled, letting it fade away as he continued to remember, putting bits and pieces of the days together.

The door. Everything seemed to lead back to the damn dungeon door. He remembered walking right to it when they got there and seeing all the debris in front of it, the bush that had been there for so long buried between the rock, wood, and rubble. He'd mentioned the second lock being off, figuring it had been broken by a falling rock from the wall above, and Mairi had looked at him like he was mad. With her forehead furrowed so deeply, her brows couldn't have gone any lower if they'd wanted to, she'd marched past him and started moving the smaller pieces of the pile.

"What are you doing?" he'd asked her.

Hands on hips after she'd tossed a stone to the side, she glared at him. "What does it look like I'm doing, dumbass?" When he hadn't answered, she'd thrown her hands up in exasperation and gone back to chucking rocks. "Seriously,

Luke? Abra was so sure Will was here. You know as well as I do that she's never wrong. We need to check and make sure he didn't try going into wherever this door leads. You said so yourself, the lock had been secure the last time you were here. Did you ever think that maybe Will broke it off, went in, and then the rocks trapped him inside?"

Luke sucked in a deep breath and let it out slowly. Of course, he'd thought of it, but something inside kept telling him not to open the door. Had he already been in the past and his dragon remembered being captive down there? Luke didn't want to consider that. If he had already visited the past and couldn't remember it, did that mean he'd forgotten about Ami as well? The thought had him grabbing the front of his shirt over his heart.

"Kiernan?"

His great grandfather in younger form turned his head in Luke's direction, a raised brow indicating that Luke should go on... another mannerism that Kiernan had retained over centuries of time. It made Luke smile inside.

"Do you... do you forget about previous times you've lived in?" he asked, knowing by Kiernan's silent squint that he hadn't expressed himself very well. "Like, when you've gone back to the past, do you remember that now?

Shaking his head, Kiernan smiled. "It's not the same for me. I was born, released my dragon, and continue to live. I don't travel around in time like you did." When he laughed and Luke didn't, he sobered. "What's troubling you?"

Luke looked away, his voice distant when he answered. "I don't want to forget her, Kiernan."

"I'm sorry, Lad. I don't know what to say."

Luke understood. There were too many unknowns, though one thing he felt for sure was that this battle they both knew was on the horizon was going to be fought in the future, not now.

The future… that's where the forces of evil had been released, and that's where they would have to be defeated. He closed his eyes for a moment and prayed. Fate had brought her to him once. Even if they did get separated, surely it could happen again.

He opened his eyes and looked at Kiernan.

"Love, my boy, is a powerful thing."

Luke nodded. *Love.* He certainly hadn't expected to find it when he'd gone to Somerled that Sunday morning. And certainly not six hundred years in the past.

Chuckling, Kiernan slowed his horse and began to steer them off the path. Luke looked around in surprise. He knew this land, though he'd never approached it from this direction.

"Tavish Manor," Kiernan told him just before they topped a hillside and could see the house in the valley below.

Luke's heart leapt at the sight of his boyhood home. "You still live there," he marveled, never taking his eyes off the house.

Kiernan smiled. "We tend to come back to it as often as we can."

With difficulty, Luke tore his eyes away and looked at his great grandfather. "So, how does that work, anyway? I mean, in my time, you're an old man, but obviously not as old as you really are?"

That made Kiernan laugh. "We're able to choose our age, though it usually coincides with the age we need to be. Like now, it was important for me to grow up with Ami and her brothers. When her grandmother was a young woman and we thought she might be the one to unlock the next dragon, I was an older man, going by a different name. And when Lady Saundra was a babe, I was in my forties." He paused. "When do you first remember Abra and myself, Luke?"

Luke thought, though it didn't take much work to remember. It was a time that had forever branded his heart. He was seven, Will was four, and Seth had just turned eleven. It was summer and his family had gone to Creighton to visit his grandparents like they always did. There was some Georgian festival they always liked to attend... Georgian, as in the time period, with all of the clothing and scenes from that era. He let out an ironic chuckle. A lot closer to his own time than this, that was for sure. Too bad there hadn't been a Medieval festival instead. Maybe he wouldn't feel like a fish out of water. Anyway, while they were visiting, there'd been a fire in the old house where his grandparents lived. His father had gotten the boys and their mother to safety and gone back in to try to save his parents. None of the three of them had come back out.

Before the ashes had even cooled, his great grandparents had showed up, the man taking charge, the woman taking them under her wings when his own mother fell apart. He looked at Kiernan.

"Where do you go when you're not living among the humans?" The question felt strange knowing he had always believed himself to be human until he found out he was a Blend.

Kiernan didn't answer for a few seconds, then he shrugged. Luke figured he realized the new dragon would know soon enough.

"We sleep. In the caves. Sometimes for decades, sometimes for just a few years. In the days of old, our ancestors might spend centuries down there."

Luke nodded. "Are there others? Still sleeping down there, I mean." He thought of the wall of dragon scales. Had that dragon been sleeping when the wall collapsed on him? That thought didn't appeal to Luke in the least. Maybe he'd just find someplace above ground to sleep, if sleep was required.

"At times there have been, though I believe the caves to be empty now, thanks to the last Dubhagan raid some two hundred years ago. I feel in my heart that there must be others, only I can't find them. Not here, anyway. Not in Lochlainn." He sighed then kicked his horse into faster motion, calling back as he sailed down the hill. "I fear there are not many of us left."

Luke clicked his tongue and tapped the flanks of his horse spurring the animal after Kiernan, then reined him back in with a chuckle when he noticed the beautiful blonde who had just come out onto the porch. With her hand blocking the sun out of her eyes, she watched the approaching riders, then let out a squeal. Luke laughed. He'd heard that sound before.

Abra.

Even in her eighties in his time, Luke had somehow known his great grandmother must have been beyond beautiful in her younger years. He'd been correct. A petite woman, slender except the rounded swell of an expectant belly, white-blonde hair, much lighter than Ami's, hung down her back in silken curls. Soft blue eyes that held a hint of mischief belied the innocent pout of her full lips. Vixen was the word that came to mind and made Luke laugh, causing her to pull away from her husband and look up at him.

"Luke Tavish," he told her as he slipped from his horse

and held out his hand.

Her whole face alight, she smiled her welcome, clasping his hand in both of hers in more of a hug than a handshake. "I know, dear. Welcome home." She laughed and squeezed his hand before turning back to her husband. "Come inside, the two of you. Tell me all about what has been happening."

Kiernan swatted her behind playfully as she scampered in front of him. "As if you didn't already know." He glanced over his shoulder at Luke, motioning the still stunned man to follow them. "It's the mind thing, remember?"

"He doesn't know as much as he lets on, Lad. It's the mind thing... and magic," she said leaning past Kiernan's arm to look at Luke. "Come on now."

Luke shook his head. Talk about surreal to see his great grandparents, the people who had practically raised him, appearing younger than he was and very much in love. He looked at Abra's pregnant belly and felt a jab of sadness knowing the baby she carried would never reach his full potential. That had to be hard on them. How many children had they watched come and go?

"You can't dwell on what ifs, Luke. All you have is what is. Be happy with that."

Wide eyed, he stared at Abra, nodding after a few seconds. Was she able to read his mind as well?

She laughed. "I can't read your mind, love. But I still know what has to be going on inside your head."

Luke laughed, thinking how in all those years she had changed so little. This Abra was the same woman who had nurtured and cared for him as a child. Smiling, he sat down in the chair she pointed to near Kiernan before she sent a servant to get them something to eat. Luke was glad. He had a feeling the afternoon was going to take an awful lot of energy that he suddenly didn't have.

The changing part, Luke quickly found out, had been a terrifying piece of cake. It was the flying that had given him fits. He was sure he'd take to it naturally, though he supposed even baby birds probably crashed a few times before finding the right lift.

"Again," Kiernan commanded after they'd changed back to human form for what felt like the hundredth time, when it had only been four or five. The shifting definitely took enough energy for it to feel like a thousand.

Luke sighed, his head dropping down, he stared at the ground for a few seconds before closing his eyes. He could feel his muscles rippling, bones changing even before he stretched out his arms, his head coming up and back. Exhilaration shot through him, his skin prickling as flesh became scales—shiny, colorful, glass-like layers stacked in an overlapping pattern. He wondered what Ami would think of him.

She'd been so enamored with the yellow and amber stones in the Room of Embers. Luke twisted his neck, looking down his long body. Not too unlike Kiernan, he was multicolored though purple, he would say, was predominant. His snout, from what he could tell, was a deep purple that faded into a dazzling blue, giving way to something just shy of turquois green before changing back to blue and fading into the beautiful purple.

When they were flying over a pond, he'd taken a moment to look at himself, noting the long, pointy horns that jutted out of his head. They'd reminded him of elephant tusks, only straighter. Maybe unicorn horns better explained them, though they were larger and sharper than he'd ever imagined a mythical creature might have.

A spiked ridge ran full length of his spine, from neck to tail. There were a couple smaller spikes in his wings, which he had to admit, were pretty spectacular. He kept thinking of that kids' movie where the one character told the other, *Impressive wing span, man*. That might not have been it exactly, but it was close enough and exactly how he felt. Standing on the ground, he flexed them a bit, wondering how anything so seemingly thin could carry something as large as him.

He looked at Kiernan who had also changed and noticed the man was softly laughing at him. Luke squinted his elliptical eyes and tried to scrunch his nose, then he laughed as well.

"So, old man. When do I get to learn to breathe fire?"

Kiernan scoffed. "Old man! Huh. At least I've been born by now." Both dragons laughed. Shaking his head, Kiernan added, "Sorry to tell you, lad, that's something that didn't get passed down. At least, I don't have that power, and the Blends I've managed to come across in my lifetime didn't have it either."

"Others?" Luke picked up quickly on the slip. "I thought you said…"

Kiernan was already shaking his head. "I didn't say there weren't others. I said there weren't any that I could find now. In all my years, I've come across a few. I know they're out there, Luke, I just don't know where."

Luke thought for a moment, then nodded, even though he disagreed. If there were others out there now, then why was it so important for him to be brought back… not that he was complaining after the night he'd just spent with his

Prihom. Luke quickly reined in that thought. Getting aroused as a human was hard enough to control, but a horny dragon... he had a feeling that was a whole other force to be reckoned with. He was thankful when Kiernan turned and, with two steps forward, took to the sky.

"Come on," he yelled back at Luke. "One more flight before we head back. The sun will be starting its descent soon and I've heard there will be a certain young lady joining us for dinner again." His great grandfather laughed as Luke growled and took to the skies again. At least concentrating on flight would keep him distracted for the next few minutes.

The ride back to Somerled was mostly quiet except when Kiernan asked him how he felt. Exhausted, Luke had told him. Kiernan laughed, telling him it would get easier. His shifting would soon be second nature. "Kind of like making love to the right girl," he'd said with a wink. "You become one and it feels right. With your dragon, you're one and the same. Once you learn to share the power, that too will feel right."

Luke wasn't sure he'd have used that analogy, though shifting from man to dragon had definitely been exhilarating, almost as much as making love to Ami, only in a completely different way. But, the being one... he liked that. One with his dragon, and one with the woman he loved.

The two men left their horses with the stable hands and made tracks up to the house just as the sun was beginning to set. At the door to the castle, Kiernan looked up and frowned. Luke swallowed hard. He'd seen it too. The dark shadows had returned and there was only one thing he could think of that they would be after.

"You can't have her," he mumbled under his breath as they went in. "She's already mine."

Chapter 13

The men were already seated around the dinner table when Lady Saundra and her lovely daughter arrived, their chatter stopping when they entered the dining room, arms linked. Ami turned her face from her mother to look directly into Luke's eyes. She let her gaze drop quickly, but not soon enough that it didn't have his heart racing and the blood rushing south at the speed of light.

Dinner, he was afraid, was going to be the death of him with her by his side. He'd already told himself he dared not touch her, because just the thought of her had the beast inside him roaring and he wasn't talking about his dragon. He could feel his skin prickling, much as it had at the manor before he'd shifted. It looked like they were both excited to see her.

When Ami approached and Kiernan stood to help her into her chair, Luke had never been so thankful in his life. Just like in Luke's own time, the old guy seemed to have a sixth sense about him. Of course he did, Luke thought. By his time, Kiernan had lived almost a millennium. If wisdom came with age, it was no wonder his great grandfather was filled with smarts. No doubt being a dragon helped too. Luke chuckled, then dared a glance to his left side reveling in the sheepish smile returned to him. It was a gesture filled with promise.

Tonight, he thought. He knew she'd received his message and its intent when she shifted in her chair after sucking in a quiet breath. He smiled at the single word reply.

Tonight.

The meal couldn't have taken longer had they had it catered, or worse yet, had to go out and kill the meat before cooking and serving it. The dishes set before him were tasty, but that was not what he was hungry for. He breathed a huge sigh of relief when, just before it was time for the women to leave, Gairlich informed them that port and cigars would be dispensed of because he had an important announcement and everyone was to gather in the drawing room at once.

"That includes you, daughter."

Ami's cheeks flamed when her father pointed a finger at her, though she managed to nod. Luke took the chance and squeezed her hand that was nestled on her leg beneath the table. She squeezed back, pulling her hand away as if the fire that had quickly spread between them might truly consume them. Clearing his throat, Luke pushed back his chair and rose to help her up, thankful again when Kiernan stepped in, offering her his arm as escort instead.

The announcement that a special license had been granted for Luke to marry Amileigh on Sunday was met with surprise by many and great excitement by the rest. Luke heard the whispered speculations that he chose to ignore even though they riled him and rankled his dragon. He looked at Ami who was shaking her head.

"Sunday?" She turned to Luke and then to Kiernan. "It will be too late," Luke heard her whisper.

Gairlich moved forward, taking his daughter by the upper arms. "Now you object?" A look of complete confusion contorted his face as he leaned toward her. "You told me before I dispatched the messenger that if I believed it was for the best, then you would concede to this plan," he whispered just loud enough for her to hear… though with their dragon hearing, both Luke and Kiernan had heard as well.

Amileigh shook her head. "No, Father. I don't object. It's just…" She looked past him, her eyes welling with tears that she quickly blinked away. "Sunday is so far away."

Those gathered around laughed, many mumbling about the impatience of young love.

"Forgive me, my Lord, but is there no way to move it to Saturday? Perhaps that would be more to the Lady's liking. And mine as well." Luke winked at Amileigh, trying to act the part of the eager groom. The room again erupted into laughter.

"I'm sorry," Kiernan volunteered when Gairlich simply frowned. "That was the earliest the Church would allow."

Clapping her hands, Lady Saundra rushed forward. "A Sunday morning wedding in the West parlor will be perfect. I can see it now, with the light shining in…" She linked arms with Ami, steering her daughter toward the exit while chattering away.

At the top of the stairs, Lady Saundra paused, looking back at the guard that was dutifully following them up the steps. She rolled her eyes then continued on, kissing her daughter on the cheek in front of her door. When Ami made to open the door, her mother held tight to her hand.

The older woman breathed deeply, plastering a smile to her face, and exhaling slowly as she turned around. "Young man," she said to the guard just before he settled into his chair. "I could use your assistance for a moment, please."

The guard looked from mother to daughter, his eyes wide. How could he refuse a command from the Lady of the

House? Saundra laughed, Ami cringing at the flirtatiousness of it.

"Oh, come now. I just need you to help me move my chaise closer to the fire. There's a chill in the air tonight and I need to write some notes to be dispatched tomorrow morning concerning my daughter's wedding. The door will be open so you'll be able to hear. I can even help you keep an eye."

After a few seconds of hesitation, the guard moved to follow, but only after Ami had opened her own door and moved as if she was going to go inside. As soon as the guard stepped into her mother's room, Lady Saundra motioned her daughter to go. Stunned, Ami quietly closed her door, walking softly to the stair landing and then sprinting to the far end of the adjoining hall. She didn't dare look back before turning the knob and slipping into Luke's room.

Giggling like a little girl, she covered her mouth, even though the room was empty. She couldn't believe what her mother had done. Walking over and picking up Luke's rose petal peach colored shirt that was draped over the chair, she raised it to her face, inhaling deeply. She moaned softly, rubbing her cheek against the material before putting it back down. With trembling fingers, she untied the bow at her neck and began to unlace the bodice of her gown, letting it fall to the ground when she was done before reaching again for Luke's shirt and letting it whisper over her as she slipped it onto her arms, unable to believe what she was about to do.

Hurry, Luke, she whispered in her mind, then she sat down in the chair, one foot on the stool in front of it, the other leg draped over the arm. She closed her eyes for a moment, trying to quell the nerves fluttering around her insides. This is silly, she thought. He's going to think I'm some immature child. She started to move and heard him growl.

"Nuh uh." He continued in a deep, raspy voice. "Don't move, beautiful. I want you right where you are, wearing nothing but my shirt." She watched him saunter toward her, slowly working at the tie at the neck of the peasant shirt he wore. Pulling it over his head, he sunk to his knees before her, leaning in to where the material of his peach shirt pressed against the apex of her legs. "And me."

"Oh Lord," she whispered.

"Oh, Luke," he chuckled, letting his head fall to where his face was nestled in the open fabric that revealed the outline of her breasts. He slipped his hands between them, pushed the material to the side, and placed his palms on her flattened belly. Ami couldn't help but suck in a deep breath, especially when his fingers began to glide upward. Her nipples hardened and her breasts were fully alert, wanting what she knew he was about to give her.

"Yes," she breathed as his palm scratched across one taut peak.

"This?" he asked, grazing her with the pad of his thumb.

"Yes," she barely managed to get out.

Luke smiled and turned his head, letting his tongue trace up the side of her breast as he went.

"Oh," she groaned when his tongue met his thumb, nearly crying out when he did it again and again.

Ami thought she might come up out of the chair when he reached down with his other hand and let his fingers slide through the wetness pooling at her center. Oh, how she wanted him!

"Luke," she whispered, straining against his hand. She

arched her back wishing he would take her in his mouth. With a chuckle, his mouth closed over her breast and he pulled away slowly sucking as he went, letting his tongue circle the silken end.

When his other thumb found its way to her swollen core, Ami cried out. He began to move it in rhythm to his tongue and slipped his two fingers inside of her. There was no doubting, Luke was an expert lover.

"Oh, Luke," she moaned softly, as her body clamped around his fingers and her world shattered into mind numbing pieces.

Ever so slowly Luke released her, even before she had stopped twitching. He stood up, scooped her limp body into his arms, and took them both to his bed.

"How long do we have?" he asked, falling in beside her.

Ami stared up at him. How long? She had no idea. "As long as you'd like," she whispered, running her fingers into his hair and pulling his head down to hers.

"How about forever," he mumbled against her lips.

Yes, she thought. Forever wouldn't be too much.

Chapter 14

Luke had just covered Amileigh's body with his for probably the millionth time that night when a loud banging sounded on the door, followed by it being pushed wide open.

"Luke, we need to get... Oh, Lord. I, uh..."

Luke craned his neck to look toward the end of the bed to where he could see Kiernan standing in the opened doorway staring at the floor. "Kinda busy." Luke chuckled when he looked back at Amileigh beneath him, her face covered with her hands. "Don't think that's gonna hide you, love," he whispered, reaching down to deliver a playful nip to the back of one hand. She glared at him though her fingers and he rocked his hips causing her to suck in a deep breath.

"So, I, uh, so I see. Well," Kiernan cleared his throat. "When... when you're done, could you, uh, come next door and get me?"

The door closed with a thud before Luke answered.

"When we're done," Luke chuckled. "He may be waiting a while." He feigned hurt and laughed when Amileigh slapped him. He leaned down and ran his nose against hers. "You're adorable when you blush, did you know that?"

Ami rolled her eyes. "Get off me, Luke. I need to leave." She tried to squirm away from him, but Luke just pressed her more firmly into the mattress.

"He said when we're done." Luke wiggled his hips again. "I don't know about you, but I..." He paused his words while beginning to move inside her again. "Am not done." He raised a brow. "Are you?"

Ami's eyes glazed over and she slowly shook her head.

Once they were dressed, Luke pulled Ami to him, wrapping her in his arms before lowering his face and letting his lips glide gently over hers. He rubbed his fingers over the crease in her forehead. "No need to worry. I've got you, Babe. I'll just slip over and get our distraction from next door."

With Ami secured back behind her own room door, Luke decided it was time to broach the subject with Kiernan that had been bothering him.

"In my time, Abra thought my brother Will was at the ruins when he didn't come home after an outing Thursday night. He was supposed to have gone with his friends to a local pub, but when we called around late Friday, they all said he never showed. You were away, but Abra had us take her to Somerled, where we looked around, but found nothing. When we left, she didn't seem overly upset, but she didn't seem completely at ease either."

"We?"

Luke nodded. "Mairi was with us. She's..." He raised a brow, his mouth drooping downward. "I guess you'd say she's your ward. She just kind of showed up not long after we came to live at the Manor, saying her name was Mairi McCollum. No one had ever questioned it, and after seeing Amileigh's mother, I'd say that's about right."

Kiernan motioned for Luke to continue when he didn't.

"Mairi and I went back on Saturday, and that's when we noticed the lock missing on the door to the dungeon."

"The lock?" Kiernan frowned

"I know there's only a plank of wood baring the door now, but at some point between now and then, locks, two of them, were put on the door. In later years, you had locks put on all the doors of the rooms that remained intact to keep potential vandals out."

Kiernan nodded. "What about the second lock on the dungeon passage?"

"Right. Well, Will and I had found the door..." He squinted, thinking. "Wednesday, I think it was. You see, after a lot of discussion with the state, we had been given the green light to begin the restoration of part of the old castle and Will and I had been up there working. When we left, we were joking around. I shoved him and he tripped, falling through a bush and careening into the old door with a metallic bang. If he hadn't, we might have never known it was there. Anyway, we'd tried to get in, breaking one of the locks."

Kiernan raised a brow and Luke shrugged, giving him a lopsided smile.

"So, what exactly does it mean when you get a green light?" Kiernan asked.

Luke blinked a few times, running back over what he'd said. "Ah! Well, in my day, we travel by cars instead of horses, and when you come to an intersection there are lights that..." He laughed at the blank look on Kiernan's face. "Never mind. It just means we were given permission to go ahead. Anyway, the next day, which would be today, Mairi and I went back to the ruins and she made me help get all the rocks and timbers that had fallen in the last tremors away from the door. We didn't finish until close to sunset and even though she wanted me to go down and look for Will, I couldn't do it. We did open the door and call down, but there wasn't any response so I convinced her to wait." Luke looked away. "When I saw Will here on Friday morning he was... he was heading down the hallway toward the door. If Abra and Mairi were right, then he probably did go down there. If I'd gone down that Saturday, I might have been able to save him and stop all this." Luke made a circular motion in the air with his hand in front of him.

"Don't do that to yourself..."

"No, Kiernan. I have to."

"No, Luke. You don't. Did you not hear what Abra said at the Manor? You can't live in the what ifs, only on what you have now. Trust me, Luke. I've lived enough lifetimes to know that if you do, you'll be ineffective and no good to those who need you the most. Think about it."

Luke knew Kiernan was talking about future generations and those they, as Guardians, were sworn to protect, as much as he was Amileigh. Scrubbing his hands down his face, Luke blew out a deep breath. "When Mairi and I went back to Somerled on Sunday, the door was wide open even though I had pushed it closed the night before. Since I hadn't put the bar back and the locks were broken, I had shrugged it off, even following Mairi down as far as the holding room when she demanded we go down to look for Will. He wasn't there. Nothing was, except for the decaying bars of the cell. I don't even remember seeing the other door."

Luke closed his eyes, trying to imagine the room. He envisioned himself staring at the cell where he'd been held and then turning around to see the guard going through the other door. *I'll be back to take ye to hell*, the burly man had said before removing the huge bar that blocked the second door in the corner. "There wasn't another door." In his mind, he could almost make out where it looked like the upper section of the adjacent dirt wall had partially crumbled and the dirt and rocks had slid down to cover the door, solidifying over time to make it appear like a seamless, rounded corner. Luke opened his eyes and looked at Kiernan. "What's behind that door, Kiernan? Besides the criminals left down there to die?"

Kiernan shifted, shuffling from foot to foot, his blue eyes locked with those so similar to his own. He squinted, his hand coming up to stroke his chin before he sucked in a deep breath that he slowly pushed from his lungs.

"The first son was born almost nine months to the date after the union of Nicholas and Helaina, some fifteen hundred years from your time…"

"I don't have time for a history lesson, Kiernan. I already read about them in one of those big books. They got married. People were killed." Luke practically growled.

Kiernan crossed his arms over his chest and glared at his future great grandson, saying nothing else until Luke rolled his eyes and told him to go on, even though he was sure he knew everything his great grandfather was about to tell him.

"Nicholas and Helaina were believed to be the first perfected Blend and Prihom. Their union was heralded and celebrated from the time of their births. They're the ones we read about in the tomes. Only the year before they were to be married, great unrest occurred. King Nicolai's power hungry brother secretly joined forces with the Dubhagan to help them kidnap Helaina. The plan was to do it when she was escorted home after the annual Gathering of the Hearts so that she might be mated with Ekbatair Drahgan's son. He too was believed to be a most perfect Blend from their side.

"When the Dragon King announced the couple was to be married the night of the annual gathering instead of the next year, an all-out war began. Rurardi Ruthven—the King's brother, believed to be his second in command, had not even been told because King Nicolai already suspected him." Kiernan tapped his temple. "Even then, he was filled with wisdom beyond his years."

Smiling, though more from polite habit than anything else, Luke absently nodded. "Nicolai and his brother... they were actual dragons, right?"

Kiernan nodded. "It was nearing the end of the time when men and dragons walked the earth together."

"Helaina and Nicolai obviously got married though."

"Nicholas," Kiernan corrected. "Nicolai is the Kedan Dragon King. Nicholas was the perfected Blend, named after the old dragon by his father, Christos Tavish."

Luke sucked in and Kiernan nodded.

"Yes, Luke. We are direct descendants of the first perfected Blend. That's why I have always believed Fate has had something spectacular in store for my offspring, the reason I've had to fight off disappointment when my sons' Prihoms have not materialized throughout the years." He stepped forward, placing a hand on Luke's shoulder. "It's why there is no doubt Fate has something spectacular in store for you."

Luke stared at Kiernan. He wouldn't disagree. He only wished he knew what it was. "The door, Kiernan. What's behind that second door?"

Motioning for Luke to follow him, Kiernan turned toward the hallway that led to the dungeon door. "It's not the second door, Luke, for behind it lies only those who have wronged this family. What you're asking for is what you will find behind the door that's beyond that."

Chapter 15

When the guard with the missing teeth and the body filled with scars pulled open the door between the holding cell room and the beginnings of the actual dungeons, Luke was glad they had yet to eat because he was sure he would have lost it.

The stench of years of death and decay swirled around them, mixing with a hair-raising dose of pure evil. Luke could feel the goosebumps prickling his skin, the cold fingers walking up his spine. He tried not to look at the faces pressed up against the bars closed over low, floor-level openings into these dark, earthen cells, but it was hard not to. Desperation showed on some, hatred on others, and then there were those who had already checked out while waiting on a certain fated death. Luke shook his head and watched the guard kick back a bony hand that reached out as they walked by, covering his ears against the cries. The rights' activists back home would have had a field day with this, he thought.

"Lord McCollum is a fair man, Luke," Kiernan whispered. "Everyone here deserves his fate."

Luke nodded, but inside he was thinking that no man deserved to rot in a dark cell.

Kiernan knew what his great grandson was thinking. He also knew Luke may have thought differently if he'd known what some of those men had done, especially those caged behind the door at the end of the long passageway. The thought of many of those, tried and sentenced long before the current lord of the castle ever existed, had his hackles rising.

He could feel his dragon straining, his own blood boiling as they closed in on the large, triple thick, wooden structure. As the trio approached, the two men guarding the door bowed, then stepped back, each grasping hold of thick ropes hanging down on either side of the door. In perfect unison, they pulled, straining muscular torsos and arms to lift the door from the ground just enough for the three men to bend down and slip under before it slammed down again.

When Luke gagged, he turned to him, trying to fathom what all of this must be like for a man who hadn't even known dragons existed before he was sent back in time. Kiernan pulled a piece of cloth from his pocket and pressed it into Luke's hand. "Hold it to your nose. Inside, there's mint from Abra's garden. I'd planned to have it in my tea later, but I think you'd better have it." Luke nodded, holding the cloth to his face and breathing deeply a few times. When he whispered that he was okay, the trio continued.

"What is this place?"

Kiernan looked at Luke taking in the partially dug out empty caverns lining one wall of the walkway they were headed down.

"It almost looks like..." He was eyeing the small alcoves and ledges along the opposite wall, then staring up at the way the structure curved above them. "It's not manmade like the part we just came through. This... this is part of the caves below, isn't it?"

"It's the cámara da maldición de mil durmir—the chamber of the curse of a thousand sleeps." He chuckled under his breath, but there was nothing humorous about it. "I guess they were off by about a century though." When

Luke frowned, Kiernan went on. "In the battle on the night that Nicholas and Helaina were united, the Dubhagan king, Ekbatair Drahgan, was captured. The Nebrani wizards that had crossed over to their side centuries ago declared that if he was not released they would curse our people, and after a thousand sleeps, the Dubhagan would rise up, wiping out any remaining Kedan Blends, leaving them free to enslave mankind and rule the existing universe."

"But a thousand sleeps is only, what… a little over two and a half years? So how…"

"Dragon sleeps, Luke. In our time, a sleep was equivalent to a year. We're at nine hundred years now, today." Kiernan tapped his finger against the opposite hand. "Nine hundred sleeps, not a thousand. It doesn't make sense though. The timing…"

"Maybe it does," Luke interrupted. "Maybe when we found the dungeon door and opened it, something happened that set events in motion before it was time, but once they had begun, there was no stopping them."

Kiernan stared off into the darkened passageway, his hand absently stroking his chin. "What else happened when you returned to Somerled on Sunday?"

Luke thought for a few minutes. He ran over the events… he and Mairi driving to the ruins, her freaking out when the metal door was open and running down the earth-hewn steps without knowing what might be down there. He'd followed her down with the big flashlight they'd brought since he'd already told her they'd have a look, but hadn't expected her to just run blindly down into whatever lay below.

Nothing had come of that anyway, so he'd shrugged it off. When they got back up to the top, they'd decided to move some of the fallen rocks toward the back of the castle where they were working on the reconstruction of the old staircase, the one that went up to the rooms that had remained intact. It would never be a whole castle again, but using materials from the original structure on the reconstruction made it seem more authentic. Anyway, they'd moved the rocks, hopeful that by working in the area, if Will was there, they might hear him or something. Luke frowned.

"It was a sunny day, but the sun kept dipping behind the clouds, only I remember now looking up at one point and seeing nothing but blue skies for miles and miles around. And we kept hearing noises. Most of them we could explain away, but toward the end of the day, there was a strange sound on the second floor. It would have been in the section where the family's bedrooms are."

Kiernan nodded. "What did you do then?"

Luke frowned. "I told Mairi to stay there. That if someone was up there, I'd yell and she was to get the hell out of there to go find help." He bit at his lower lip. "When we got to the ladder—it was an old wooden ladder that was normally kept behind one of the partially crumbled walls. We'd put it up to gain access to the second-floor hallway. Anyway, it was already in place, only the bottom few rungs were broken and when I tried to pull myself up past them, my jean pocket caught and ripped, so Mairi told me to give her my phone and wallet." He looked down, walking through the hallway in his mind. "There was nothing amiss, no one around, nothing out of place that I could see, other than the fresh pile of empty beer bottles I assumed Will had left. The rooms were all locked up just like they were supposed to be... Wait. The weathered chair by the table across from the one room, Amileigh's room... it was over on its side so I picked it up and put it back beside the table, then climbed back down. I think both mine and Mairi's nerves were rattled so we were cutting up, trying to cover with our crazy bantering. We decided to call it a day. That's when we rounded the corner and ran into Amileigh."

"What was the sound that caught your attention?"

"The sound?" Luke frowned. "Huh. There was a thud and then something that almost sounded like a muffled cry followed by... a dragging sound. I think." Luke shrugged and Kiernan held up his hand as they neared a slight bend in the tunnel and Luke stopped talking. He was surprised to see another set of bars blocking their way and was thankful for his dragon-bred night vision, because the closer they got to those bars, the more the hair stood up on the back of his neck. He didn't want to walk into anything he couldn't see, that was for sure. He jumped when the guard who had escorted them down jangled the keys attached to his belt, pulling them loose and sorting through them before plunging one into the lock on the entrance in the bars. After turning it, the screeching sound of the old lock making Luke cringe, the guard handed the keys to one of eight other guards standing at attention outside the smaller tunnel and motioned for Kiernan and Luke to go through. Luke would have given anything to have remained where he was, especially when both Kiernan and the guard unsheathed their swords.

The sounds of dragging chains, moans, growls, cursing, and crunching bones began to fill the air as the bars swung shut behind them. Luke's eyes widened as they walked along the corridor that began as a narrow passage before widening into a hallway similar to the one they'd just passed, with the jutting rocks and alcoves on one side and the large, open chambers on the other. Only these chambers weren't empty.

"This is the actual sleeping chamber," Kiernan whispered. "There are many chambers like this in the cave where the Kedan Dragons would come to sleep... a hibernation of sorts, only different than what animals experience. Some of these sleeps would last for a few years, others for centuries, depending on the needs of the dragon and the command of the Universe. They were used as a time of healing and restoration, and for the imparting of wisdom."

Luke nodded, still trying to take it all in. He was overwhelmed by all he still had to learn.

"When the need to expand the dungeons led to them stumbling on the part we just left, no one thought too much of it. They were, after all, just empty spaces, albeit strange to those who had no idea what they were. Still, few know of the existence of this place, and even less are the numbers that have any idea about the existence of dragons. The men you saw as we walked down, myself, Gairlich... Thankfully, Carvic here was in charge of the excavation, and as soon as he realized what they'd hit, he came to me.

Luke scratched his head. "So, you just dug through a wall and there was this passage?"

The guard who now had a name turned to look at Luke before grunting and turning back. Luke raised a brow and Kiernan chuckled quietly.

"It took nearly a year, but yes. They had to clear part of the passageway from debris and fallen chunks of earth and rock, but they found this second part by chance."

Chance? Luke doubted that. None of this seemed anywhere near left up to chance. "You seem to know a lot about the battle. How did you not know where this Chamber of Curses was?"

"We did. Or they did... our ancestors. Only they

accessed it from below. At least they did before it was believed to have collapsed. The old Dubhagan King and the others imprisoned with him were assumed to have perished, not too unlike King Nicolai's brother in the Room of Embers." Kiernan shrugged. "We know that at least a third of it did collapse, and no one expected that the chambers would ever be accessed again. It simply wasn't considered."

"Wow." Luke realized his head was pounding badly. He'd have much rather this venture stay within the confines of his trip back in time and the enjoyment he found with Amileigh. He'd even settle for having found out he was a dragon, but to learn there was a curse and all these captured dragons could rise up against them was more than he could process. *Them*, Luke thought, currently consisted of him and Kiernan... daunting. "How many are down here?"

Kiernan answered without hesitation. "Twelve. Four actual dragons and eight Blends. Unfortunately, three of them are our own."

The realization of Kiernan's words met him along with the first occupied cavern. Standing in the middle of a double cell, a man with a large chain attached to his leg stared back at them. He looked way too much like Will. Luke felt his heart sink to the pit of his stomach as he started to step toward the bars. Kiernan grabbed hold of his arm and he stopped, turning to look at him.

"He's broken free of those bars twice now, Luke. He may look like one of our kin, but his heart is pure Dubhagan."

Luke nodded, continuing to stare at the man, realizing the low growl was coming from him. He wondered what the man had done to earn him his fate, considered asking Kiernan, then thought better of it.

"Why doesn't he just turn into a dragon and escape his

cell?" Luke asked instead.

Shaking his head, Kiernan motioned for Luke to follow. "Our magic requires light in order for us to change, therefore, those captured as dragons, remain dragons, unless they change before we can get them down here. Those who are in human form, will remain in human form. It's partly why we have the thick wooden door at the end of the other chamber. The distance and the door keep the light from reaching down here, and should one escape and make it that far, the width of the door should keep him in."

They passed by several more similarly caged men before the wall curved out and a very different sort of cell came into view. Behind a triple barrier of bars at least as thick as a man's arm, a huge beast loomed, froth dripping from his mouth, his eyes red and wild. When he growled and snorted, the breath that blew in their direction had Luke returning the mint infused cloth to his nose as he fought the urge to gag.

The creature pawed at the ground, making the floor beneath them shake, leaving them on unsteady feet for a moment, especially when his great tail collided with the wall of his barrier. Straining toward the bars, the dragging sound of a heavy chain was followed by the clank of it drawing taut, the long neck whipping around to look down to the clasp around his leg. He howled and bucked and Luke found himself stepping back, even though the barrier should have made him feel secure. Did he look this frightening, this huge in dragon form? He'd viewed himself as beautiful when he'd flown over the pond. Certainly, there was no beauty to the beast in front of them.

"Come on," Kiernan whispered. "He'll settle once we're past."

Luke couldn't move fast enough for his own comfort,

though he quickly stopped when a few short feet down the passage, they stepped in front of another cell similar to the one they'd just left. Only its occupant nearly broke his heart. The dragon inside lay peacefully toward the back wall, its majestic ivory head curled over its massive paws. Luke was startled when the beast blinked and even more so when he noticed the color of his eyes.

"He's one of us?" Luke asked, his mouth and brows both drawn down.

"Don't let him fool you, Luke. Captured just a couple of years ago, he too is Dubhagan through and through after selling his soul to the dark dragons."

The beast chuckled, still not raising his head. "You make it sound so ominous, Blue Eyes."

"You chose the wrong side, Branco."

Kiernan's response elicited another chuckle. "We'll see. Lore has it we are to come out the victors, completely annihilating your breed and making mankind ours to do with as we please. No more of that weak species dictating what we can and can't do." He lifted his head and stared down at the trio. "Is that the wrong side, or the right?"

Kiernan motioned for them to move on, mumbling something about wisdom and stupidity.

Luke glanced back, saw the expanding chest as the huge beast sighed before plopping its head back to the floor. He'd chosen poorly, and the worst part was that no matter what he said, the Blend in dragon form knew it. Just like humans that get caught up on the wrong side and can't change even though they want to. They weren't so different after all. He thought of a conversation he and Kiernan had earlier.

We're really not so different—dragons and humans. Our emotions, our likes and dislikes, our sense of self preservation and the desire to protect those we love... Really, it's mostly just the desire to prepare and cook our meats instead of eating them straight off the kill, and their mounting of their women from behind. Luke had nearly choked on his own spit on that one. Clearing his throat, he'd looked down and laughed when Kiernan added, *And I'm guessing that choice is obviously debatable.*

Damn. He'd rather be with Amileigh trying out that thought. He shook his head and moved on, sucking in his breath in awe as they moved to the next cell, and the next, and the next one. Huge beasts, every bit as loathsome as the shackled dragon only larger... much, much larger, slept in the caverns toward the end, their large bodies taking up the majority of each room. Luke wondered how they could sleep through the commotion.

A thousand sleeps. Kiernan's words echoed in his mind.

Luke should have kept his thoughts of their impressiveness tuned down a bit, because nothing could have prepared him for the sight in the last cavern before the passageway ended. Impressive shades of black, glass-like scales shimmered even in the darkness around the dragon that was larger still by at least six to eight feet. It was hard to tell since he too was laying down, his body relaxed in a state of sleep.

The horns protruding from the massive head weren't white and unmarred as Luke's had been. They were crooked and chipped, some broken, as were many of the spines along the ridge of his neck and tail. This dragon had seen many battles... *and loved every one of them*, the voice inside Luke said. With every breath, the air recharged with the darkness that was in the old dragon's heart. Luke could feel it winding around him, trying to find a way in. He shuddered, drawing Kiernan's attention.

"Come on," the old man in his younger body whispered. "Let's get you out of here."

Gladly, Luke thought with one last glance at the dark king sleeping behind thick bars.

As they passed the others, Luke couldn't help but look at them. He found himself pulling up short in front of one of the smaller, double layered cages. Frowning, he looked at Kiernan. "Isn't that the man who was after Amileigh in the forest?" Kiernan nodded and his frown deepened. "We thought you'd killed him… you washed the blood from your blade in the Room of Embers."

"Wounded only before dragging him here. That's what took me so long. I wanted him alive so I could question him."

Luke nodded slowly, looking at the battered body of the man. "Why didn't he change back into a dragon? It was daylight out."

"The wounds," Kiernan told him. "You can't change once you're wounded to a certain degree either." He sighed. "Obviously, he refused to speak, even after a royal beating. We even threatened to put him in with the mad dragon down there." Kiernan cocked his head in the direction of the dragon who had slung slobber their way while rattling his chains.

The dark Blend would have probably welcomed that as certain death. "How many others do you think are out there, Kiernan?" he asked as they walked back to first the metal gate, and then the wooden plank.

Kiernan shrugged. "It's hard to tell, but obviously they still have those who have yet to transform. Otherwise they wouldn't have such a need to possess Amileigh." He looked at Luke and chuckled. "Only now, she's not much good to them, is she?"

Both men chuckled and Luke could feel the heat returning to his body. He may have spoiled her usefulness to the Dubhagan—she may not be any good to them, but she was certainly good with him. Damned good. Hands down, the best.

At the top of the dungeon stairs, Kiernan paused, telling Luke to take a few minutes to wash up and change. Luke agreed, more than ready to wash off the stink of nearly a thousand years. When his stomach growled loudly, Kiernan laughed and told him to meet him in the dining hall. They'd eat lunch before heading out to the training field. He felt a wave of disappointment. It looked like there would be no flying for him that day.

Too bad he was wrong about that.

Not even an hour into their training, the shadows began and Luke noticed the others with them seemed to notice them as well, unlike the times before. He looked at Kiernan who seemed remiss to put an end to their session and hightail it back to the castle. He kept reminding himself that Amileigh was safe inside, her guards having been increased to the one outside her door and one watching each staircase, just as an added precaution before the wedding, at Kiernan's request. Luke tamped down his worry... or tried anyway. Concentrating on his training, he seemed to be succeeding until the whoosh of wings and the startled cries and commotion from his companions had him feeling the spines of his own dragon nudging against his back.

"Kiernan!" he yelled above the hubbub of the men running toward the canopy of the nearby trees.

Kiernan was shaking his head. "Not yet, Luke. Wait..."

A roaring screech and screams from the midst of the men changed everything in a split second as one of the dark beasts swooped in, his massive head swinging, sending men flying even as they stopped to wield their swords against the glass-like plates of the armored body.

"Kiernan!" They looked over to where Amileigh's oldest brother had dropped down beside Auley, blood soaking the younger man's shirt. They ran over just as another shadow swooped in. Grabbing the wounded man, the other warriors protecting their backs, they ran the last few feet for the trees. When they settled him, Luke ripped off his shirt, pressing it to the gash across Auley's chest.

"Damn," Amileigh's twin cussed. "That's two of my shirts down." He tried to laugh, ending on a sucked in breath and a wince.

"It's not bad," Luke told him, pulling the shirt back so he could see. "You're going to hurt like hell, but you'll live." He was glad. He'd grown to like the younger man over the last few days.

Standing, the oldest McCollum brother moved to the edge of the trees and was almost pushed back by the edge of a swiping wing. He turned to stare at Kiernan. "I can't have my men or my family jeopardized by this insanity any longer, Kiernan."

Nodding, Kiernan stood after administering a reassuring squeeze to Auley's shoulder. He stared out, watching the shadows move over the field before them. "Luke."

When Kiernan motioned him over, Luke stood as well. He could feel the nerves working on his stomach.

Head close, Kiernan told him in a low voice, "There are three. At least. I believe there could be another waiting out of sight, but I'm not certain. I could handle two, maybe three, but not four." He paused, looking down before locking eyes with his future great grandson. "They need to get Auley back to the castle. If he's not treated quickly, a deadly infection could set in." He looked over his shoulder. "I didn't want them to know... all these years I've walked in their midst, my true identity hidden from most of them, believing that was for the best."

Luke nodded, wincing when another roaring shriek came from the sky, his mind turning to Amileigh. She must be terrified. Swallowing hard, Luke turned to Kiernan. He may not be ready, but what choice did he have? What had Kiernan said about the likenesses of humans and dragons? Something about their desire to protect those they love. Dragon or man, Luke felt an urgency to protect the woman he loved as well as her relatives and those who served them. "I'll follow your lead, Kiernan. Let's do this."

Amidst cries of protest and affirmation that they were madmen, Luke and Kiernan stepped from the protection of the trees. Arms out to the side, they began to run, both men changing, transforming into beautiful, multicolored beasts. He could hear the gasps from behind him, even over the shrieking cries above. Pull your head into the game, he told himself. This wasn't the time to dwell on anything other than the fight.

"Go for the neck," Kiernan yelled, nodding toward one of the smaller dark dragons coming at them from the side. "Just under the head. And get him on his back if you can."

Luke wasted no time, knowing Kiernan would hold off the others as long as he could, but with their size, he'd soon need help. Best to get this one out of the way. He shot upwards and then dove down, circling his confused opponent before climbing again and repeating the maneuver, only this time, when the beast raised his head,

Luke lunged, his huge jaws closing over what had to be the only tender flesh on the whole creature. When the dark dragon lashed out, his claws scraping against Luke's less armored belly, he sunk his teeth in and bits of scale and blood filled his mouth. Cheers from below fueling his fury, he lunged forward, flipping his opponent onto his back. A great moan of defeat filled the skies as the beast screamed.

Behind you, Luke. Look out!

Ami! Of course, she could see from the castle. Luke hated that she had to be a part of any of this, and yet he was doing it for her, to protect her and the future of the Kedan Blends. He crunched his jaws tighter before releasing his prey and pulling back just in time to fend off an attack from another dragon that dropped over the trees. The fourth dragon that Kiernan had suspected. For the future... his future, and theirs.

Sheer will and forty minutes of time had him and Kiernan dropping back to the earth, both heaving for breath for several seconds before their dragons melted back into man form. Luke bent over, his hands on his knees as he glanced around at the four dragon bodies scattered across the field. He'd never worked so hard for anything in his life.

You're beautiful, dragon man, he heard in his head. *Truly amazing.*

Luke smiled. *And my dragon side isn't so bad either, is he?* He heard Ami's laughter in his head just before he and Kiernan were swooped up by the cheering men.

At the door of the castle, Auley called to him.

"If you weren't already marrying my sister tomorrow, you know I'd have to challenge you on the fields, don't you?"

Luke offered a lopsided smile before nodding. He was so tired that the wounded man could have most probably done it, too. His mind was too tired to play games.

Auley faked anger before laughing. "That's what I thought." The younger man sobered. "Do right by her."

Luke ignored the threat, knowing he had no intention of doing anything else. He looked up, his heart clenching when he saw the woman in question standing at the end of the hall. Without a word, he started walking toward her, picking up his pace when she began to run, his arms going around her waist when she didn't slow and their bodies tangled as he spun her in a circle. Her hands in his disheveled hair, she pulled his face to her, covering his mouth with her own and coaxing his lips open with her tongue. From the gasps he chose to ignore he guessed public displays weren't something common in medieval castles. He heard the cleared throat of her father and started to pull away, only to be stopped by another voice.

"Let them alone, Gairlich," Lady Saundra admonished her husband. "Do you not remember being young?"

Still kissing their daughter, he cut his eyes to see them as they walked by, Gairlich still mumbling, his wife's head leaned against his arm that she hugged. She winked at Luke and he couldn't help smiling.

Amileigh pulled back, staring up at him through lowered lashes. "May I have the honor of helping you bathe your wounds, my Lord?" she asked sheepishly.

Blinking, Luke grabbed her hand and turned toward the back stairs knowing if they didn't hurry he might just take her right there on the floor.

Amileigh had dinner sent up to them, claiming the soreness of her companion from his battles and her unwillingness to leave him as their excuse not to join the others in the dining room. She laughed when the portions sent up were enough to have practically fed him in dragon form and the staff who delivered them were eager to quickly leave them. Their lack of being disturbed otherwise led her to believe her mother had obviously found a way to occupy her father as well. Popping another grape between Luke's teeth then leaning in to bite it in half, she smiled while she chewed. She'd have to find a way to thank her.

The daylight beginning to stream through his window had Ami scampering away from Luke's room, her insides jumping with giddiness. In just a few hours, they would be married, joined together for all eternity.

We already are, he'd told her during the night. Ami supposed if she was being honest with herself she'd have to go further and admit that not only were they, but they always had been. It wasn't often that Fate reached down and stirred the pot of time to bring couples together who were separated by six hundred years.

A knotted fist grabbed hold of her inside. She didn't want to think about that because if it could happen to bring them together, it could happen again causing her to lose him.

"What's wrong, Milady?"

Amileigh's head snapped up when Abigail entered her room. When her smile faltered, the maid came to stand beside her putting an arm around her shoulder in a manner that most servants wouldn't have dared.

"So much has happened in such a small amount of time, Abigail." She blinked back the tears that filled her unusual lilac eyes. "It's not every day the man of your dreams comes out of nowhere."

"And then ye find out he's a dragon," Abigail added with a chuckle.

"Yes." Amileigh laughed. "Who would ever have thought..."

Her words trailed off as the light in her room changed. She frowned. "Did you see that?" she asked, walking toward the window.

"See what?" Abigail was already moving toward the wardrobe. "Your mother sent over a dress last evening for you, she did." The maid pulled a white gown from the cupboard, her hand stroking down the length of silken material before she laid it on the bed.

With another look out at the sunny sky, Ami moved to join her maid, her heart pounding as she stared down at the gown. "'Tis beautiful," she confirmed. She knew this dress. It was the one worn by her mother at her own wedding, and her mother's mother before her. She fingered the delicate beadwork along the hem. Sucking in a slow, deep breath, Ami blew it out loudly and walked away to stand before the still opened wardrobe. She reached up, pulling out the dress she'd worn on her ride with Kiernan, the one Abigail said she had yet to wear.

Turning, she looked at her maid. "Put it away, Abigail. I intend to wear this one."

The shock on her maid's face when she changed into her own white gown was equaled only when she demanded a simple braid draped over one shoulder for her hair.

A girl only gets married once in a lifetime, if she's lucky, Abigail had told her, trying to urge her to play up the part of the maidenly bride. Ami had refused, standing firm in her decisions even though her heart longed to wear her ancestral dress and to let her maid pile her hair, adorning it with jewels fit for a lady being married inside castle walls. The only concession she made was when Abigail brought her a small box.

"This isn't a part of your wardrobe," the maid told her. "Your mother said to tell you it's a gift… something that has been passed down from generation to generation, since the beginning of time."

Amileigh ran her fingers over the long, wooden box. It looked old, weathered, and opened with a creak to expose a pendant hanging from a simple chain. She touched it, fingering the gold wire that wrapped precisely around the rough stone. The imprecise edges only added to the overall beauty of the piece. Lilac, she thought. Just like her eyes or… the color of Luke's lightest scales. The stone, no bigger than her smallest finger, was stunning, commanding in its simple beauty. She held it up for Abigail to help her slip it on. With a smile, she dismissed her maid and sat down in the chair near her window. There was nothing to do now but wait.

Kiernan should have known there was something amiss when he received the note from Luke asking him to meet him in the Room of Embers. The cryptically written message had said something about getting one of the scale pieces as a gift for Amileigh since she'd seemed so taken with them when they were all there. Rereading it while he waited in the empty chamber, he realized it hadn't actually said that last part, he'd just surmised it through the chicken scratch.

"Damn," he huffed, realizing their victory the day before had made him lax, not to mention Abra's coming in for the wedding. He'd shocked a lot of people with the fact that he was married, but he was tired of hiding on all fronts. Now, he wasn't so sure that all his actions were so well thought out. Acting before one thought was never a good idea.

Just as he turned, the hair on the back of his neck stood on end. He reached for his sword, but couldn't unsheathe it before a hard object coldcocked him, causing him to stumble forward a few steps before he hit the ground.

Ami didn't move when she heard the scuffle outside her door. She'd known they would be coming, she just wasn't sure how, or when. Her heart beating against her chest, she closed her eyes imagining herself riding across the open field with Kiernan. She'd looked back when the dark beasts screeched and watched Kiernan morph into a beautiful dragon. Only it wasn't Kiernan. It was Luke.

"Luke," she whispered, as her door flew open. She stood quickly, coming face to face with Batair Draghan.

"Amileigh McCollum," he ground out, looking her up and down. "You would have saved us all a lot of trouble if you'd just married me years back."

Luke's dragon felt Ami call him. Not the same as when they used their mind speak, but more her heart crying out to his. He stood, ignoring the scowl from her father on the other side of the desk where they'd been having a *man-to-man* in his study.

"Something's wrong," he told the chagrinned man. Not waiting for a response, Luke stormed out of the room yelling to the servant at the far end of the hall to get Kiernan. He tore up the back staircase, stopping short when he saw the bloodied bodies of the two guards laid out on the floor in front of Amileigh's room. He'd always wondered about the dark spot there, imagining it had been caused by the outside elements, but never blood.

"Ami!" he screamed, stepping over the bodies and pushing open her door, already knowing the door would be empty. He fought against the men who had rushed up behind him... Gairlich, Auley, Amileigh's other brothers. Back in the hall, he looked up to see a wide-eyed Abra. "Where's Kiernan?" he asked, his voice breaking with the anguish.

Pulling her wrap tighter around her shoulders, Abra's eyes pleaded with him, even as she answered. "He went down to the cave... to meet you."

Luke had never moved so fast in all his life. He grabbed up a sword from one of the fallen guards and flew to the stairs. He heard Gairlich barking orders to his sons and the other men who had already begun to assemble, but he didn't wait, instead bursting out the East door, coming to a halt just past the exit to the rose garden. He stood in the yard, his chest heaving as he looked around, realizing he had no idea at all where they would have taken her.

Kiernan. He had to find his great grandfather. Abra had said he went to the cave, but which way? He tried to listen, to sense Ami, but there was nothing, until he was hit with a sudden burst of yellow light. He could see Kiernan laying on the floor, the wall of water cascading behind him.

"Hold on, Ami," he whispered before he began to run.

The trek down to the Room of Embers took a lot less time than it had the day he, Kiernan, and Ami had walked from it to the house. He'd thrown caution to the wind, the visions flashing through his head showing bits and pieces of the cave, a rather large man grunting in what could only be an angry pursuit, and darkness. She wouldn't have his night vision, and if the man was a Dubhagan Blend, he would. At least Luke suspected as much. He touched his chest over his heart to quell the hurting. It didn't help. He could sense her fear.

"Kiernan!" He knelt down by the man he would one day call his great grandfather, the memories of his life with the older man on fast forward playing in his head. Tears welled in his eyes as he reached out a shaking hand, working up the nerve to feel for a pulse.

Sucking in a ragged breath, Kiernan turned his head. "Go," he croaked out, one finger on the hands crossed over his chest pointing to the center passageway leading from the Room of Embers.

Standing, Luke looked down at the man who had yet to move more than just enough to let him know he was alive. "Don't leave me, old man. I'm going to need you, you know."

Kiernan coughed on a chuckle and Luke squatted back down. "I'm not going anywhere. History's already proven that," he managed in a raspy whisper. "Go, Luke. Find her."

Luke covered the hands over Kiernan's heart with his own and squeezed. *I'm coming, Ami,* he thought before standing up and taking off down the middle corridor at an all-out sprint. They were too close to the cave's exit. Through her vision, he was starting to see bits of light.

"Luke!" Ami heard him coming and screamed, barely able to lunge forward beyond the grasp of the man who had killed her guards and tried to take her hostage. He'd almost succeeded, but when she'd delivered an unexpected blow to his manhood, he'd dropped to the ground, losing his hold on her. Ami had seized the moment, surging forward into the forest instead of turning back to the house. If she could get to the caves, Kiernan had showed her all the best places to hide. Only she hadn't counted on seeing Kiernan laying there near the pool in the Room of Embers, blood oozing from a cut to the side of his head. His hands had been placed over his heart much like they were for the dead.

She'd frozen, staring at her old friend, willing his chest to rise to alleviate her worst fear. It hadn't happened. Or maybe it had and she just couldn't tell. The sound of footfalls behind her had spurred her forward. She could almost hear Kiernan's voice in her head telling her to run, that if he was dead, her getting herself caught wasn't going to bring him back. So she had run, though her gawking ate away at her precious lead and Batair had almost caught her twice. Only her better knowledge of the caves had saved her, allowing her to zig and zag through some of the narrowing corridors. But he was closing in on her. She could feel the heat of his body as he lunged for her. His hand grazed her back and knocked her toward the rocky wall of the cave. She went down and he was on her, pinning her arms above her head with one hand while the other closed around her throat.

"Back off, Tavish. The girl's ours." He leered down at her. "I've waited a long time for this." He leaned toward her and Ami whipped her head to the side just before his mouth found hers. Batair tightened his grip on her throat and she sucked in a raspy breath.

"Get off her, you evil freak."

Luke. She tried to focus on the direction his voice had come from.

Batair laughed, the smell of his breath making her want to gag. "You truly are stupid, aren't you? Did you really think I'd just up and let you have this lovely Prihom? Do you think I don't know who you are?" He ran his nose along her jawline and Ami whimpered. "I don't need her, but we have plenty of Blends who would gladly sink themselves into something as pretty as this." He shook his head. "Go back to the future, *boy*," he growled. "I'll kill her before I give her to you."

His hand against her throat growing tighter still, Ami could feel her world beginning to spin.

Stay with me, Ami, she heard in her head just before Luke's laughter rang through the passageway.

"Boy?" Luke laughed again. "I don't hear any respect in those words, Bait Ear. Is that the best you've got?"

The dark dragon Blend growled at the jab.

"Maybe what you really need is for someone to teach you a lesson. I'm pretty sure I kicked the ass of one of your kin in the future," he lied. The reality was, the Hagan boy had honestly gotten the better of him, but he wasn't about to let this evil bastard know that. "Why don't you get up from there and let's have a go. Show me what you can do against a man instead of a helpless girl."

Batair laughed, easing his hand back as Ami went limp. He pushed himself to his feet, towering a good four inches over Luke. "You should have just given me the Key, Tavish." He shook his head, taking a step forward. "Your kind is always the same, letting your heart get in the way. But you want to know what I'm going to do with your heart? I'm going to crush your chest and eat it. And then I'm going to take your girl and watch as one of my brothers…"

Ami winced when she heard the bones of Luke's hand connect with those in Batair's jaw. She rolled toward the wall, thankful Batair had fallen for it when she'd faked that she'd passed out. A few more minutes of his hand on her neck and she'd have been out for real. She managed to duck into an alcove just as the dark Blend spread out his hands, his body slowly shifting from man to beast. With a low growl, he bared his teeth, his massive tail slapping against the floor of the cave. "The girl belongs to us, Tavish. She is our key."

Luke's laugh caused goosebumps to ripple down her arms. He sounded so ominous as he stepped back, his gaze traveling from the dark dragon's head to the tip of his tail. "Sorry, Batair, but I'm afraid you're wrong."

If a dragon could have crinkled his forehead in confusion, Batair's surely would have been. He snorted, his deep voice boomed in the cavern as he questioned Luke's comment. "Wrong? About what?"

"The girl. And me." Luke took off toward the opening of the cave, the sunlight glistening on his skin. He had to know the dragon would follow him, just as he'd surely known he couldn't win in a fight against Batair as a man. As he ran, he transformed. "Sorry, *old man*." He whipped sideways, slamming Batair into the cave wall. "She was my key, and now my tail's bigger than yours."

Roaring, the huge beasts lunged, the sound so near that of glass crashing together it forced Ami to cover her ears. Wings tight at their sides, they rolled, first one and then the other ending up on top. Crushing bones and anguished cries mixed with the echoes of footfalls. Ami could see the armed men from the castle coming down the passageway, Kiernan balanced between one of her brothers and her father.

Dear Lord, she prayed when Batair once again flipped Luke to his back, his huge head seeking access to the delicate flesh at the top of his neck. *I need him. We need him.* She covered her belly with her hand. She must be carrying his daughter for the dark dragon to have sensed a pure Prihom. She closed her eyes, imagining the three of them walking along the banks of a quiet pond.

"Luke!" someone called.

She heard the castle guard rush forward, opened her eyes as the man she loved stepped back from the dark dragon laying lifeless on the cave floor and transformed. When she stood, he staggered toward her, his lips twitching in what she'd assumed was an attempted smile. Their arms found one another and he stumbled, spinning them so that it was his back that collided against the wall. He let his head loll back, closing his eyes as Ami kissed his neck.

Her tears on his chest caused him to open his eyes.

"Hey, Baby." His chuckle turned to a moan that he stifled before bringing his hand up to caress her tear streaked face. "Man, this dragon shit is hard work."

Ami laughed, stroking his cheek and pushing up on her toes to press a kiss to his bruised mouth. "You were magnificent."

A cleared throat had them turning toward the group of men gathered around the lifeless body on the ground. Gairlich frowned at them. "I believe your mother is waiting," was all he said before he skirted past the dead dragon and marched by his daughter and the man she loved. Ami looked at Luke and both had to stifle their laughter.

"You have greatly chagrinned my father," she whispered, kissing him one last time before easing back and taking his hand.

Luke nodded, pushing away from the wall with a groan. "And not for the first time, I'm afraid."

At the entrance to the cave, they surveyed the skies, seeing nothing until they neared the castle entrance. The fighting men having gone around to a back door, the family made a mad dash up the steps that would lead them into the grand entry hall when the shadows appeared following a rolling earth tremor. Luke squeezed Ami's hand noting the tremor in her lips when she tried to smile.

"What the hell?" The earth shook violently beneath them, their world dissipating into ripples not unlike he'd seen the morning he'd watched Will climb down the ladder from the battered second story.

"Luke!" Mairi's voice cried out to him.

Squinting, he could see her, barely, her hazy form turning in a slow circle as the room morphed back and forth between the ruins and the grand castle. He could hear the roaring screech above them, the dark shadows falling over them each time the room shifted to ruins. He looked around to where the others stood, their eyes wide, though no one moved.

Mairi screamed just as one of the dragons swooped toward her and Luke yelled at her to get down. She managed to duck low, barely escaping the grasp of one of the great beasts and backed up against the wall just in time to ward off another attack.

"Mairi," Luke whispered, reaching a hand toward her only to have her fade before returning again seconds later. He looked up at the solid structure above him and shook his head. He couldn't see them, but he could hear the roars and cries. The dragons hadn't stopped. They wouldn't. They needed her more than ever to help them complete their quest. He looked at Ami when she squeezed his hand.

"You have to go," she whispered. "You have to help her."

Taking both of her hands in his, he turned to face her, their eyes locking. "Come with me, Ami."

She looked around at her family and Kiernan. She shook her head. "I can't, Luke. This is my world."

Ami watched Luke's chest rise and fall, his teeth grinding. She could see the anguish in his eyes as he looked from her to where Mairi huddled against the wall crying out for help.

"You're wrong," he ground out, turning back. "*I* am your world, as you are mine."

She shook her head again, tears welling in her eyes. "I'm sorry. I can't go."

Cursing under his breath, Luke finally nodded. He'd told her once before that being with him had to be her choice. Pulling her to him, he kissed her, his mouth taking hers in a passionate plea for a lifetime. He stepped away. Blinking back tears, he whispered, "I love you," and took the coin from his pocket. He ran his finger across it and started to fade. "If you change your mind," he called, tossing the coin toward her as the ripples overtook him.

"I'll know where to find you," Ami finished on a sob, watching the coin fall to the ground.

The sound of the spinning coin was deafening in the silence. Ami turned, looking into the faces of those she loved. Her parents, her brothers, Abigail, Kiernan... how could she leave them?

She placed her hand on her stomach. How could she not?

Lunging forward, she grabbed the coin before it reached a full stop. "I love you, too," she whispered, closing her eyes.

The sounds of screeching cries, claws grazing the broken walls of her ancestral home replaced the silence. Ami opened her eyes to see Luke and Mairi standing much as they had when she'd first seen them.

"Luke!" she screamed. "In here." She waited for them to run across the foyer and the three of them slipped into the hidden alcove just as another of the dark dragons swooped down, his cry at having lost his prey echoing through the empty halls.

Pressed together in the tiny space, Luke stared down at her for several seconds before placing his palms on either side of her face. "You came," he whispered.

Ami smiled up at him. "I couldn't imagine living a lifetime without you by my side, or raising our child alone."

Luke's mouth crushed over hers, his hands moving down her backside, pressing her to him.

"Uh, I don't know what the hell's going on here, and I'm guessing congratulations are in order, but I think maybe you two ought to put that off until you can get a room. In case you haven't noticed, there are freaking fantasy beasts flying around out there trying to kill us!"

Her forehead dropping against Luke's chest, they both sort of half laughed. When Luke moved to step away from her, Ami tightened her arms around his waist. "Don't go," she whispered looking back up at him.

He sighed and kissed her forehead. "I don't see any other way." His smile was sad. He looked toward the opening of the alcove. "Damn. I sure wish Kiernan was here."

Mairi covered her ears as one of the beasts screamed from somewhere above them. The shaking of the earth followed a loud thud and a triumphant roar.

"I think your wish has been granted," Ami told him, stepping back and giving his biceps a squeeze.

"You stupid ass! You're going to get killed if you go out there," Mairi yelled when Luke moved toward the opening of the alcove.

"He'll be okay." Ami took hold of Mairi's arm, the younger woman looking at her like she was mad. "I think there are some things I need to tell you..."

Three dead dark dragons, a few superficial wounds, and an hour and a half later, the four crawled into Luke's old work truck and headed for Ruthven Manor—Tavish manor in Ami's time, only she'd never seen it before. She wasn't sure about the ugly carriage that pulled them along and kept asking how it worked without horses.

Later, he'd find her in front of the television, her mouth open as she watched the *strange box with the oddly dressed people in it*. He wasn't sure how many times she got up to look behind the thin screen. The running water and the electric lights in the house amazed her as well, and Luke thought how much easier it had been to go back in time than it must be for someone to come forward.

He at least had history to go on. That had given him a mostly accurate accounting of what was happening in the past. Ami had learned via Kiernan that her family had all gone on to live long, productive lives inside the walls of the castle. He'd even taken her to see their graves at the family cemetery. She'd cried that night after walking among their headstones, running her fingers over the chiseled dates, though she'd assured him they were not tears of regret.

As for Somerled and how it fell into such disrepair, they'd found nothing on it in the archives. Kiernan knew, and Abra, though they both told them it was a story to leave for another day. Suspicious, Luke had thought, but he knew them both well enough to know neither of them would budge until they were perfectly ready.

He wondered those first few days, worried about the

dragons beneath the ruins. He and Kiernan had shored up the metal door shortly after the last of the dark dragons had fallen the night they'd returned. Together, they'd gone back down to assure the passageway to the cámara da maldición de mil durmir remained blocked. It had, and the following day they'd gone into the caves, searching for a way into the chambers from inside. The only one that could have been it was so clogged with debris Luke guessed it would take a sonic blast to break through.

Or an earthquake of notable size.

He'd ignored that voice. Since they'd shored up the door, there'd been no sign of even the slightest of tremors.

When they'd emerged from the cave, Will was waiting for them. Luke smiled, clasping his brother on the back.

"The ladies have gone shopping," he told them with an exaggerated eyeroll. "I overheard them chattering about Amileigh's need for a trusseau, so I hope that card you handed her has plenty of money on it."

Chuckling, Luke shrugged. "Providing she can even figure out how to use it." They'd all laughed then.

Luke stretched, yawning as they walked toward the parking area. This had been one hell of a week. "Hey," he said to Will as they approached the old truck, "did you walk out here? That's quite a haul."

Will shook his head, his dark hair swishing around his eyes. He pushed it back from his forehead. "Are you kidding me? I had the girls drop me on their way." He huffed. "I've done more than enough walking to last me a lifetime."

Luke had worried about Will the whole time he and Kiernan were barricading the dungeon door. He couldn't shake the feeling that his brother was still out there, but he hadn't said anything to his great grandfather until they were mortaring in the last rock.

Kiernan had looked up at the fading sun, his smile widening as his gaze veered off in the direction of the old training field. He shook his head and laughed. "Right on time," he'd said pointing at the faint glimmer of a distant light. "Just like Will to show up once all the work is done."

They'd waited, watching the light grow brighter and two figures materialize behind it. Luke felt sure his eyes were as wide as his mouth as he took in the woman beside his brother, her attire unmistakably Georgian. He remembered it from the festivals they'd attended in Creighton when he was just a kid.

Kiernan just smiled, leaning in to hug the girl before clapping his great grandson on the back. "Welcome to the twenty-first century, Brinna. Could have used you a little earlier, Will."

When Luke asked him where he'd been, Will had laughed. "You're never going to believe this…" he'd started.

There was a time Luke wouldn't have.

Chapter 16

"It's a lovely day for a wedding, isn't it, my dear?"

Ami jumped, startled that Abra had managed to get so close without her knowing. Both women laughed—something Ami was surprised to find herself doing often during the three months she'd been in this different time. Perhaps she belonged here after all.

"Your mom would have been so proud." Abra reached up and pushed a strand of blonde hair back behind Ami's ear, much as her mother might have done.

Ami smiled, her lips trembling with her effort to hold back the unwanted tears.

"I think she would have wanted you to have these," Abra told her, pulling the bouquet of ribbon tied flowers from behind her back.

Ami sucked in a deep breath, staring down at the flowers—a sweet mixture of roses and daisies with stems of sweet mountain cranberries strewn through the middle. Her eyes traveling upwards, she saw it then, the stone around Abra's neck. It wasn't quite like the lilac one she wore, but still similar with its deep purple, a hint of green and blue around one edge. Abra winked at her and turned to walk away.

"They smell like love," Ami had called to her.

"Yes," Abra had answered without turning back.

Luke had never seen anything as lovely as the woman who walked toward him, her arm laced through his great grandfather's. He smiled at her as if the moon had just hung the most beautiful star in the sky. He was glad she had asked that they be married in what remained of her family home. It almost had the feel to him that her family was actually there, and Luke liked that. He sensed their approval, had every time he'd seen the ripples and spoke into the silence that he was doing his best to take good care of their Ami.

Their Ami. *His* Ami.

Luke thought about the day they'd taken her to see her old room. She'd wandered around, picking up her belongings, quickly replacing them all until she opened the wardrobe. She'd sucked in, a drawn out oh whispered on a sniffle. She'd stroked the yellowed dress, rubbing it against her cheek before reaching up to pull it free.

"My mother's wedding dress," she'd told him. "My great grandmother's as well." She laid it across the discolored coverlet on her bed. "I want to wear it."

Luke had looked over his shoulder, questioning Kiernan with his eyes. Since the ruins had been deemed a historical site, he wasn't sure if they could legally take anything away. He'd smiled when the old man had nodded, thinking how it was as difficult for Kiernan to refuse her anything as it was for him to do so. They both loved her, in very different ways.

He noticed the beads in her hair that she'd pulled from a box hidden beneath the fake bottom of the wardrobe chest. If he had to wager a guess, they weren't beads at all, but rare jewels, maybe even chips of dragon scales.

"What else do you have in there?" he'd asked when she'd reached back in for the third time. She'd needed two hands to pull out her last find. It was the book—the tome that had gone missing from her mother's room. He'd reached for it and she'd pulled it away.

"It's for Abra."

Both he and Kiernan had stared at her, their mouths

gaping. "But... why?" he'd finally asked.

"Because we were meant to live the future, creating it as we go, not follow a script. There are things in there none of us need to know. And, if I had to wager, I'd say it's subject to change. It's written in ink, not stone, you know."

She'd laughed when he'd scrunched his face and he'd looked over his shoulder to see the exact same expression mirrored by Kiernan.

She hadn't let them see the tome either, giving it directly to Abra herself. She'd refused to let it go until it was placed with the others behind the locked doors. Luke didn't know when Abra had gained possession of the others, but now she had them all.

"Let's get this show on the road!" They all turned around to see Luke's oldest brother Seth walking up from the manmade drive. "Damn!" He shook his head, rubbing a hand over an ear exposed by his close-cropped hair. "What's with that humming?"

Luke looked at Ami and then at Mairi who stood with her hands pressed to the sides of her head, her gaze leveled on the ground at her feet. He waited, his heart speeding up as he willed her to look at his brother. They were the last ones. With their union, the circle would be complete.

Standing in the midst of Somerled ruins they all swayed as a tremor rolled the ground beneath their feet for the first time since the night Luke and Amileigh had returned.

An Deireadh
The End

On Wings of Fire
Book 2 in the Lochlainn Guardian Series

What happened to Will Tavish? Where was he all those days, and who was the oddly dressed woman who was with him when he returned to the Somerled ruins?

Find out in *On Wings of Fire*, Will and Brinna's Saga, coming soon

Stay informed at LindaBoulangerBooks.com

Or follow Linda on her Amazon Author Page
http://www.amazon.com/Linda-Boulanger/e/B002NPYDC6

While each book in this series is a complete story about the main couple, they are all a part of something bigger: The Lochlainn Guardians Series. For maximum enjoyment, I recommend reading them in this order:

On Wings of Time: Luke and Amileigh's story
On Wings of Fire: Will and Brinna's story
On Wings of Courage: Seth and Mairi's story
On Wings of Forever: The final story
On Wings of Love: Kiernan and Abra's story
The Gift of Eternity: Nicholas and Helaina's story (this is a companion novelette)

On Wings of Love and *The Gift of Eternity* could easily be read at any time, though I recommend it after the first book—*On Wings of Time*.

Author Note

I hope you enjoyed Amileigh and Luke's story. I have several people to thank for providing the opportunities for me to bring it to life. First, Julia Mills—author of The Dragon Guard Series and so many other wonderful stories. Thank you for inviting me into the Stoking the Flames author family and providing me with the wings I needed to fly when I made that leap. To my daughter, Nicole, for asking a crazy question once upon a time. "If you had magical powers and you didn't know you had magical powers, would you still have them?" Yes, that was the working of a twelve-year-old mind. Yes, I knew even then that questions would someday be the impetus for a story. To my sister, Jackie, for looking at me with hopeful eyes when I told her about Ami meeting Luke in his timeperiod and she said "but they will be going back to her time, right?" How could they not?! To both of my sisters for their encouragement… I still can't believe I wrote *that* word and that we talked about it via text! To my editor, Grace Augustine… Thank you for your input and guidance. Even beyond your professionalism, your encouragement means the world to me. To Patrick Sipperly and M.M. Roethig… You two put up with me through this whole thing. 2,000 words. 18,000 words. 50,000 words. The End! Thank you both. To my Stoking the Flames Dragon Sisters… I am so in awe of each and every one of you. I love the bond that has developed thanks to this amazing experience called the publishing of a box set. I can't wait for winter! And to those of you who took flight with me into this story of the Lochlainn Guardians, you are the true dream makers.

If you'd like to stay informed about new releases, promotions, giveaways, etc. first, consider following me on my Amazon author page and/or my BookBub page. They will notify you when a new book comes out, though my New Release and Promotions Only newsletter is the best place to stay in the loop. I don't send out a lot... usually one and sometimes a couple a month. I do, however, almost always have some sort of giveaway going for my newsletter subscribers. Sometimes the giveaway is a free book, or an Amazon Gift Card, book swag, jewelry pieces, stuffed animals... you just never know. But you can enter for your chance to win monthly by subscribing to my newsletter:

www.lindaboulangerbooks.com/newsletter-sign-up.html

The newsletter is a great way to keep informed... So is joining my Linda's Dragon Guardians Group on Facebook. You can find the group at this link:

https://www.facebook.com/groups/664151640414859/

Until the next story…
Thank you for being a part of my dream,
Linda

Works by Linda Boulanger

Novels/Novellas
On Wings of Time
Dance with the Enemy
Beyond the Shadows
Arms of an Angel

Mini-Novella
A Warrior's Christmas Gift
Makinna's Secret

Anthologies
Echoed Heartbeats
Time Out on a Roller Coaster
Becoming…
Whispered Beginnings

Color Illustrated Children's Book
When Sadie Learned to S.M.I.L.E.

Short Story Trios and Singles
Up to Bat / Center Stage / Best Friend Rules
Face of an Angel / Life Changes / Talk with Me
Secret Shame

Coming Soon/Works in Progress
Temptation's Whisper
(A Land of Riandus Novel)
Dark Warrior
(Set in the Land of Riandus)
The rest of The Lochlainn Guardians Series
(dragons and time travel)

About Linda Boulanger

Linda Boulanger is a happily-ever-after author, wife, and mother of four human children and two fur babies. She has an eclectic mix of published books, numerous story singles and short stories in a few group anthologies, plus a slew of always evolving works in progress.

Along with being an author, she designs book covers for herself and others through *Tell~Tale Book Covers* and *TreasureLine Designs*, all from her desk just north of Tulsa, Oklahoma.

Other place to find Linda:

Website
www.LindaBoulangerBooks.com

Blog
writersshelflife.blogspot.com/

Facebook
www.facebook.com/TheShelfLifeOfLindaBoulanger

Email
lindaboulangerbooks@gmail.com

BookBub
https://www.bookbub.com/authors/linda-boulanger

Amazon Author Page
www.amazon.com/Linda-Boulanger/e/B002NPYDC6